Keeping THE COWBOY

BLACKWATER RANCH BOOK FIVE

MANDI BLAKE

Keeping the Cowboy
Blackwater Ranch Book Five
By Mandi Blake

Cover Designer: Amanda Walker PA & Design
Services
Editor: Editing Done Write
Ebook ISBN: 978-1-953372-06-2
Paperback ISBN: 978-1-953372-08-6

Acknowledgments

This book had so many helpers behind it. I'm not a homeschooling mom, but I have so many friends who are and were willing to provide feedback. Thank you Hannah Jo Abbott, Tara Grace Ericson, Elizabeth Maddrey, and Jess Mastorakos for sharing your knowledge of homeschooling in four different states.

I would also love to thank my beta readers who shaped this story into something much better than what I had initially written. Pam Humphrey, Kendra Haneline, Tanya Smith, and Jenna Eleam all provided the best feedback to make the end result.

I'm extremely thankful for Margaret Amatt's extensive knowledge of the Scottish school systems. She was kind enough to share her experiences with me and helped me brainstorm this story from the beginning.

As always, I'm thankful for Brandi Aquino at Editing Done Write and Amanda Walker for their editing and cover design. These stories would be lifeless without you.

I also thank you for reading and taking a chance on this book. I love writing, but it would be nothing without readers like you.

Contents:

Chapter One

JADE

Jade stood outside her car at the Quik Stop and looked down the straight road that would lead her to Blackwater Ranch. She needed a fill-up, but she also needed a breather. Her nerves hummed and her heart beat faster with every mile she drove toward her new home.

Sitting in the car for hours did nothing to expel the energy. Fortunately, the anxiety was temporary. Jade loved packing up, moving to a new place, and starting over. There was a thrill behind the stress that made the sweaty palms worth it.

The pump clicked when the tank was full, and she set the nozzle back into the holder. It felt good to stretch her legs, but the jittery nervousness coursing through her veins told her she needed to run a few laps around the parking lot. She'd probably get a few sideways looks if she started jogging in circles.

Settling into the driver's seat of her minivan, she closed her eyes and filled her lungs with the sweet air that smelled like her favorite air freshener—heather and bergamot. The scent reminded her of her grandparents and the Scottish Highlands.

Jade pushed the breath out slowly, counting to five before opening her eyes. She picked up her phone from the console and checked her email. Still no word from the job notification site.

Some days, she felt as if she might have a shot at landing the job she wanted on the other side of the world. Other days felt a lot like grasping at smoke. Jade had spent almost every summer with her parents in Fort Augustus, Scotland visiting her aunt and grandparents, and a huge part of her heart still ached to mingle her passions—teaching young kids and living in the Highlands.

Closing out the email app, she called her mother, who had asked for a check-in when she made it to Blackwater.

Her mom answered on the second ring. "Hey, sweetie. You there?"

"Almost. I just stopped for gas, but I'm only about ten miles out." Jade started the car and made sure the Bluetooth had connected the call to the speakers in her minivan. She wiped her clammy hands on her jeans before gripping the steering wheel at ten and two.

Yes, she was a single woman with a minivan. Jade had planted herself firmly on team minivan when she started homeschooling her four nieces and nephews. It just seemed wrong to sell the Honda Odyssey that the kids had appropriately named the magic school bus.

"Call me tonight. I can't wait to hear about it." Her mother's excitement was genuine, but there was an unspoken sadness hidden beneath the words.

Jade had lived in half a dozen different cities and towns in her life, but she'd been living within an hour's drive from her parents for the last two years. Her relationship with them had only grown stronger lately. Now, she was starting a new job two hundred miles from home, and the change was bittersweet.

"Any news?" her mother asked.

It was her daily check-in. "Any news?" meant, "Have your prayers of becoming a primary school teacher in a quaint Scottish town come true?"

Jade looked right, left, and right again before pulling out onto the straight road. "Not yet."

"Don't worry. God has a plan."

"I know." Jade smiled. She heard those words so often from her family. Why was it sometimes hard to believe them?

She did know God had a plan. She just sometimes wondered if God's plan was for her to be a tumbleweed for the rest of her life, blowing where the wind took her.

"You've got this. This job sounds perfect for you. Who knows, maybe you'll love it in Blackwater."

Jade could hear the unspoken ending of that sentence. *"And you'll forget all about the Scottish Highlands."*

"It's like you don't know me at all." Jade's mother *did* know her better than anyone in the world. Her mom was also worried that Jade wouldn't find her place in the world.

When her American mother fell in love with her Scottish father in Edinburgh back in the 80s, they'd thought long and hard before ultimately deciding to live in the States. But even after Jade and her sister were born, they made a point to visit her dad's family in Scotland at least once a year.

Fast forward a quarter of a century, and Jade still didn't know which country to call home. Dual citizenship only made the distinction less clear.

"I do know you," her mother sweetly said. "And I know you're great with kids. This is where your heart calls, and I hope you love it. There. I said it. I hope you're happy enough with this job to put down roots there."

Jade tried not to read too much into the words, but her mom had summed up every doubt that hung around in the back of her mind. She *did* love kids, and she *did* want to be happy here.

"Maybe I should just forget about Scotland. It's a long shot anyway."

"I didn't say forget about it," her mother said in her no-nonsense voice she reserved for gentle lectures. "I just hope you can stop thinking about it long enough to enjoy the present. You're always waiting for the next thing."

Jade's navigation system dinged, letting her know she needed to turn soon. "I need to go. Looks like I'm almost there. By the way, this town is gorgeous."

"Isn't it? Your father and I visited Jackson Hole when we were newlyweds. It was beautiful."

The green summer fields that rushed up to the distant mountains looked similar to the

Scottish Highlands. "Gorgeous. I'll have to send Gran some photos. She won't believe how much it looks like home."

There it was again—confusing home with a country where she didn't have an address.

"I have to run. Don't forget to call me. Love you."

"Love you too, and I won't forget," Jade promised before disconnecting the call.

She turned onto the dirt road where a hanging metal sign with a backward B rested flush against an R. Both letters sat boldly within a horizontal oval with Blackwater Ranch lining the top curve.

The landscape was breathtaking. Jade had seen a lot of beautiful places in her life, and this view had her easing off the accelerator to take it all in. The drive split off to the right and left just before a large, wooden house that sat atop a slight rise.

Jade parked the minivan next to an older truck just in front of the porch that ran along the entire front side of the house. Before getting out, she lifted her phone and snapped a few shots to send to her mom and gran.

After sending the photos, Jade grabbed her messenger bag and stuffed the phone into the side pocket. The adrenaline coursing through her body had morphed from heavy anxiety to hopeful excitement. She'd looked up the ranch on the internet, and though the photos on the website were stunning, they couldn't possibly capture the awe she felt as she stepped out of the minivan.

Jade looked back at the path she'd just driven and let her gaze travel slowly over the reaching acres of the ranch, turning in a complete circle before stepping up onto the porch. The sign on the door read, "Come on in (but wipe your boots first)."

Jade grinned down at her black flats. She wasn't in Kansas anymore, or Missouri where she'd lived for the last few years.

She pushed open the solid wooden door and hefted the strap of her bag more securely on her shoulder. The room was huge with high ceilings and a rustic aesthetic that reminded her of the comfort of The Four Winds, the restaurant her grandparents owned in Fort Augustus. The mantle above the fireplace even resembled one she'd seen at a lodge in Glencoe once.

A door on the other side of the room opened, and a smiling woman wiped her hands on her apron. "Hello. Welcome to Blackwater. Are you checking in?" the woman asked kindly.

Jade rubbed her thumb against the underside of her bag strap. "Actually, I'm Jade

Smith. I'm supposed to be meeting Aaron Harding. He hired me to teach his son."

"Oh!" The woman's eyes widened, and her mouth formed the perfect O. "It's wonderful to meet you. I'm Anita Harding. I'm Aaron's mother. Levi's grandmother."

Jade relaxed as Anita's warm welcome settled around her like a fuzzy blanket. "It's a pleasure to meet you."

Jade held out a hand to shake, but the sweet lady cradled it between both of her hands and squeezed before going all in for a hug. "We're so glad you're here. We love our Levi so much, and I'm glad he'll get to start school here with you."

The gesture was so casual and familiar. Did Anita greet all strangers this way? If so, Jade was on board. It was clear Anita radiated joy as the faint lines on her face fell perfectly along a pattern that mimicked a smile.

Anita pulled back to look at her watch. "Aaron should be here any minute. I'll send for Levi too."

"Thank you. I don't mean to rush anyone. I can hang out here until they arrive." Jade gestured to the round wooden tables scattered throughout the room that surrounded a long rectangular table with bench seats on both sides.

Another woman stepped from the kitchen carrying a wicker basket of cleaning supplies with rags stacked on top.

"Laney," Anita called. "Do you have a minute to come meet Levi's new teacher?"

The woman set the basket down and eagerly rushed over. "Hi, I'm Laney. It's great to meet you." She extended a hand to Jade.

After Anita's friendly greeting, Jade hadn't known what to expect going forward. She grasped Laney's hand and gave it a good shake. "I'm Jade."

"Oh, I know who you are," Laney said. "We're a pretty close-knit bunch around here, and Aaron told us *all* about you after your phone interview."

Taken aback, Jade wasn't sure how to take the comment. Were they good things? Mr. Harding had seemed straight-forward and a little unsure on their phone call. Was he second-guessing his decision to homeschool? Had his wife insisted on the homeschool path?

Suddenly, doubt seeped into the cracks she'd begun sealing with the ladies' friendly welcome.

Laney rested her hand on Jade's shoulder. "Only good things! We were all impressed with your resume, and he said you were very nice on the phone."

With Laney's reassuring gesture, the tension eased from her shoulders. Kids were so much easier to connect with than adults, but Jade felt a comfort born of normalcy here.

"I can't wait to meet Levi. What's he like?" Jade asked.

"You'll love him," Anita said. "He keeps us on our toes around here."

Laney grinned. "He does."

"Is he the only child here?" Jade questioned.

"He is," Anita confirmed.

"For now," Laney said before quickly snapping her mouth shut.

Anita turned to Laney with a stare that could melt metal. "Spill it."

Laney's eyes grew wide, and she held up her hands. "Nothing. I-I was just assuming."

Jade heard the door open behind her, and she turned to see a broad man wearing a blue flannel shirt hang his hat on the hook by the door.

Her mind felt blank. She couldn't register anything beyond the handsome man walking toward her. She wasn't some meek kid in high school, but apparently this man was capable of making her forget her birth date and phone number. Wait, she *really* needed to remember her phone number. It might come in handy.

Anita stepped up beside Jade and held out a hand toward the man. "Jade, this is Aaron, Levi's dad."

"Oh, wow." The words were out before she even registered the sound of her voice betraying her muddled thoughts, and embarrassment sucked the breath from her lungs for a heart-pounding second. "I mean, hi. I'm Jade." She cleared her throat and tried to regain some shred of dignity after swooning over the man.

"Aaron Harding. It's nice to finally meet you in person."

Even his voice sent a comforting lick of warmth up her spine. She accepted his outstretched hand and every sensory receptor on her skin zinged when they touched. Oh, she was in trouble. She enjoyed the feel of his strong, calloused hand wrapping around hers way too much.

Of course, this seemingly awesome job wouldn't work out for her. That would be too easy. There was no way she could work for this man without fumbling around like a baby deer all day. How unprofessional. She should probably just nod, smile, and wave good-bye as she left the way she came in.

Aaron ran his fingers through his dark hair, doing little to tame it.

It didn't matter. The man could be bald, and she'd probably still melt when he looked her way.

Speaking of looks, those grass-green eyes were strikingly beautiful.

Oh no, he was looking at her, and there was too much silence. Had he asked her a question?

"Hmm?" Maybe she needed to just leave now before things got worse.

Aaron rubbed a hand over the back of his head. If she didn't know better, she'd think he was nervous too.

"Did you have any trouble finding the place?" he repeated.

"Oh, no. My GPS brought me straight here."

"Good. I have a few papers for you to sign, and then I can show you around."

Jade nodded, unable to look away and incapable of saving face. "Okay."

Rapid, low beats on the hardwood floor drew Jade's attention from her ridiculously handsome new boss, and her puppy-love session took a direct hit. A little boy who could only be

Levi barged in with a gorgeous brunette close behind.

"Shoes!" Anita shouted, stopping the boy in his tracks.

The boy turned on a dime and disappeared out the door, but the woman approached with a kind smile.

Probably Aaron's wife. That would be the icing on the cake. She'd just drooled over a married man. Good thing she hadn't unpacked. Maybe she could excuse herself to the restroom and sneak out the back door.

Why was she so nervous? She'd had plenty of jobs, attended three different colleges, and visited fifteen foreign countries. She should be a pro at adapting by now.

The little boy was back, running full speed in his socked feet past the woman. He didn't slow his run as he barreled into Laney's arms.

"Hey, kid." She squeezed the boy tight.

The woman who arrived with the boy reached out a hand to Jade. "Hey, I'm Camille, Levi's aunt."

Oh, good. The roller coaster of emotions was plummeting again. Up, down, up, down. Jade wanted off this crazy train.

She took Camille's hand and tried to catch her breath. "I'm Jade."

Aaron cleared his throat. "Levi, this is Mrs. Smith."

Jade spoke quickly without thinking. "It's Miss Smith."

Well, her embarrassment wasn't complete unless she made it abundantly clear she was single. "I mean, I don't mind if he calls me Jade."

Levi smiled up at her, looking so much like his dad. They had the same eye color, which meant she'd be spending a whole lot of time with a little reminder of her new and inappropriate crush.

"You're pretty," Levi said.

And every doubt fell away. Every thought of skipping out and forgetting about this job disappeared as she was reminded of her purpose here—to teach a young child with love and kindness.

Everyone chuckled at Levi's sweet honesty.

Camille offered Levi her fist to bump. "That's what I'm talkin' about. Nothing tells the truth like kids, drunk people, and yoga pants."

Even Jade laughed. Levi sure knew how to break the ice.

"I think we're going to get along just fine," Jade said.

She couldn't leave now. Not after meeting Levi. How irresponsible would it be to lead him to believe she'd be teaching him only to run off minutes later?

Jade looked from Levi to Aaron who grinned at his son. This man was trusting her to be a good example for his kid, and she couldn't let him down.

Everything might work out. She could give herself a pep talk tonight and push a silly crush and her lingering insecurities aside. She might like working here. Possibly a little too much.

Chapter Two

AARON

Aaron had never been prouder of his son than he was right now. The kid had a knack for saying the right thing at the right time. While Aaron had gone with the boring and safe option of asking Jade about her drive, Levi barged in with a compliment that transformed her expression from guarded to warm.

Now she was looking up at Aaron with a smile he'd be dreaming about later. He'd have to thank his son.

Levi was right. Jade Smith *was* pretty—something Aaron hadn't expected.

He hadn't really thought about what she might look like. She'd impressed him on paper first. He'd known she was the one as soon as he saw her resume.

The one for Levi. She was the one for *Levi*.

Then, she'd sold him during the phone interview. She was patient as he read the questions from the list Camille had given him, along with a full background check that showed nothing. Jade Smith didn't even have a traffic ticket on her record.

He barely remembered her responses from the phone call. He'd been hypnotized by her sweet voice—the one she no doubt used to make wild kids listen to her.

He'd been caught off guard when the woman who probably drove the minivan parked outside turned out to be gorgeous. Even though he knew she was young, he'd envisioned a middle-aged nanny with graying hair and a wooden ruler she used to pop unruly students on the back of their legs.

She was definitely not the nanny he'd expected. With short blonde hair and light blue-gray eyes, she looked like she belonged in one of those rom-com movies Camille and Haley watched all the time, not on a ranch educating his son.

Aaron was attracted to the nanny, and fate was cruel.

Not that he planned on getting caught up with another woman. His ex had left a wildfire in her wake, thoroughly scarring him.

Yet here he was, about to be wrangled into a *working* relationship with the hotter, sweeter version of Mary Poppins. Would a spoonful of sugar help the bitterness go down?

Camille's voice pulled him out of his daydream. "Levi and I are taking some food to the Lawrences. We'll be back for supper."

Aaron snapped back into the present. "Right. I have a few things for you to sign, and then I can show you to your cabin."

"Great." Jade turned back to Levi and waved. "See you in a bit."

Levi wrapped her legs in a quick hug before darting for the door.

"I think he likes you," Camille said.

Great. Aaron liked her too. Too bad it wasn't appropriate to throw his arms around her the way Levi did.

When everyone had shared good-byes, his mom disappeared back into the kitchen, and Aaron was left standing with Jade—the new nanny who made him hot and cold at the same time. Maybe he was getting a fever. That would explain the sweating.

"The office is this way," Aaron said as he indicated the short hallway near the stairs.

"So, the guest rooms are up there?" she asked as they walked past.

"Yep. There are four guest rooms plus the master. We've stayed busy since Haley took over the bed and breakfast website and advertising."

He opened the office door and waited for Jade to enter first. It was a small room with a desk, two chairs, a filing cabinet, and a bookshelf.

"Who is Haley?" Jade asked as she sat in the chair across the desk.

"My sister-in-law. You'll meet her at supper tonight. Actually, your cabin used to be hers before she married Asher. They're living in his cabin now, but they're planning on building something a little bigger soon."

"There are a lot of people here. Are they all family?"

Aaron stepped behind the desk and grabbed the folder of documents Camille had given him. "Mostly. I have four brothers and a cousin who live and work here. My brothers all have either wives or girlfriends who work here too. And Jameson works part-time, so you'll see him around.

"Wow. It must be nice being so close to family."

He stepped around to Jade's side of the desk and opened the folder. "It's nice. They help out a lot with Levi. I couldn't have done it without them."

And now was the time to stick his foot in his mouth. Jade would no doubt have questions about Levi's mother.

Before she could ask, Aaron pointed at the first page. "This one is for taxes, and the others are just your information to have on file."

Jade looked up at him with the sweetest smile. What had he done to deserve that?

"Can I borrow a pen?"

Oh, she was just being polite after he'd neglected to give her all the materials she needed.

"Yes. Here." He grabbed a pen from the other side of the desk and handed it to her in a rush.

"Thank you." She focused her attention on the page of words in front of her.

Now what was he going to do while she read every word before signing on the dotted line. Because she *would* read the whole thing. Of course, she was smart and responsible like that. She was shaping young minds. He could hear his eighth-grade teacher, Mrs. Mathews, lecturing him on the importance of the written contract.

Aaron rested his back against the doorframe. It was definitely creepy to watch her, so he focused on a knot in the old wooden floor. He snuck glances her way every few seconds.

Time was moving impossibly slow as Jade read the documents. She caught his attention every time she twisted the pen between her fingers. She moved constantly. If she wasn't fidgeting with the pen, she was twirling her hair around her fingers. The small strand went over her index finger and around her thumb, then under the middle one. By the time she finished signing the papers, he'd memorized the pattern of the strand around her lithe fingers.

"There you go. Do you need anything else?" she asked as she handed him the papers.

Aaron pushed off the doorframe and took them. He'd give them to Haley to file away. She and Laney pretty much ran the office around here. He tried to stay out of it as much as possible.

"Nope. That's it. I can show you around the main house before I take you to your cabin."

"That sounds perfect." Jade stood and slid the strap of her bag over her shoulder.

Aaron left the folder of papers on the desk and motioned for Jade to exit first. "We can start this way." He jerked his head to the left, indicating the way they'd come in. "It's pretty simple around here. The main house is where we have all meals. Yours are included."

Jade stopped in the hallway. "Meals *and* housing? That's… generous."

"It's easier that way. Mama likes to cook for everyone, so we just make it a community event around here."

Jade matched his pace as he walked. "Your mother is so sweet."

"That she is. She'll want you to call her Mama Harding. Everyone else does, and it makes her feel important." Aaron immediately added, "And she is. This place couldn't function without her."

They made their way throughout the main house as Aaron pointed out each room. Having something to focus on besides Jade's eyes made talking to her much easier.

He needed to get comfortable around her and fast. They'd be seeing a lot of each other, and things were bound to get weird if he kept staring at her.

When they'd made the circle of the main house, Camille and Levi still weren't back from the Lawrences'.

Aaron stopped when they'd completed the full-circle tour. "This is the meeting room. It's really the dining hall, but we've always talked shop after meals."

"That's interesting. Do the bed and breakfast guests eat here too?" Jade asked.

"They do. They can choose to sit with us or use the other tables we put in. They usually want to tell us about what they did that day or talk to us about what we're working on. Since this isn't an actual dude ranch and we focus more on the working ranch aspect, they can choose to tag along on our workdays or go horseback riding with Lucas and Maddie. Those two spend most of their time in the stables."

"What an amazing way to learn about the ranching lifestyle. I love it."

Aaron watched her as she studied the room. She painted the walls with the strokes of her gaze as they moved swiftly back and forth.

"Aaron."

He jolted at his mother's call. How long had he been staring at Jade?

"Ma'am?" He really hoped she hadn't already said something that he missed because he was too busy daydreaming.

The top half of his mother's body was sticking out the door leading to the kitchen. "Camille said she and Levi are staying at the Lawrences' for a while. They might hang around for supper."

"Thanks. I'm about to take Jade to the cabin."

His mother shooed them toward the door. "See you later."

When she disappeared back into the kitchen, Aaron asked, "You ready to go?"

"Sure."

"You want to follow me over? I can help you move your stuff in and then bring you back over for dinner."

Jade looked around as they stepped out onto the porch. "Is it far?"

"No, but it's quite a walk. You could do it if the weather is nice, but I wouldn't recommend going out after dark without a weapon."

"Oh. Is it dangerous?" she asked with a hint of worry in her tone.

"It can be." Aaron slipped his feet into his boots. "Better safe than sorry. If you need to go out at night, just call me, and I'll go with you."

"Thanks. It might take me a bit to get used to living here."

"I'll show you around the ranch tomorrow." He pointed east as they approached their vehicles. "The cabins are just over that hill."

"Okay. See you there."

Aaron settled into his truck and made a mental list of things Jade would need to know. If she planned to take Levi out on the ranch, she'd need a weapon, preferably one she was comfortable with. He'd need to have that talk with her soon. Even if she intended to stay close to the main house, they might still run across coyotes or mountain lions from time to time.

He parked in front of the vacant cabin and met Jade at her minivan. It would take a while to get used to seeing a minivan on the ranch.

"Where are your bags?" he asked.

Jade jerked a thumb over her shoulder. "I have a few boxes and suitcases in the back."

Aaron followed her and hefted a suitcase out of the back while Jade grabbed a box. "I'll come back for the rest after you decide where you want them."

Dixie, the ranch's helpful border collie, darted out from behind Micah's cabin and ran straight to Jade.

"Who is this?" she asked excitedly. "Is she friendly?"

"That's Dixie, and she's as friendly as they come."

Jade smiled and squatted next to Dixie, awkwardly balancing the box she carried. "I'm excited to have a dog around. I haven't been able to keep a pet recently. My nephew is allergic."

"Levi and Dixie come as a set, so I'm sure you'll get enough puppy love."

Jade scratched the underside of Dixie's throat. "We're going to be best friends. I have to go now, but I'll be back for more snuggles later."

From the porch, Aaron pointed to the cabins lined up in a row to the right. "Mine and Levi's place is next door. Asher and Haley are in the one beside you on this side, and my brother Micah is in the next one over. You can knock on their doors if you need anything and can't find me."

Jade didn't respond as he opened the door. There was a good chance she might be overwhelmed by the names he'd already thrown at her.

He let Jade enter first. "Haley just moved out of this one a few months ago. We installed the internet connection for her, but you still don't have TV."

Jade turned in a circle, taking in the small space. "That's okay. I'm glad to have the internet though. I have some online resources I plan to use for our curriculum."

Right. She was about to talk about homeschool stuff, and he was about to show his ignorance.

She turned to him with a renewed brightness in her eyes. "Have you chosen a curriculum yet?"

"Well, no." Aaron rubbed the back of his neck. "I was hoping you'd have a suggestion."

"Oh, sure! We can look through some now if you have time."

That excitement he'd glimpsed when she met Levi was back. Jade certainly loved her job. If he'd had doubts about hiring her before, they were slipping away.

"Let me bring in the rest of your stuff, and you can show me." He left the suitcase in the small living area before going back to her minivan to grab the rest. Two trips later, he'd brought in the last of the boxes.

"Thank you so much." She sat down on the couch and opened her laptop.

It looked like they'd be having this meeting on the couch. He didn't want to read too much into it, but it would've been a lot easier to focus on his son's education if he wasn't sitting thigh-to-thigh with Jade.

Stalling, Aaron looked around. "You want me to put these somewhere else?"

Jade didn't look up from her computer. "No, they're fine right there. Thank you so much."

Aaron would never list stalling as a skill on his resume.

Without another option, he dropped the boxes and sat on the couch next to Jade, careful to leave a hand's width between them.

"What are some of the things you'd like to focus on in Levi's education?" she asked.

Aaron thought about his son. He couldn't think of any area where he was outright struggling. "I want it to be fun. He likes learning, and he usually picks up on anything I teach him after watching me do it."

"So, he's an active, visual learner?"

Aaron scratched his jaw. "That sounds right. I'd like for him to be able to spend time outside. He's used to being with me or someone else out on the ranch most days."

"That's wonderful you get to spend so much time with him. Kids like to be included. It helps them learn how to make independent decisions if they're able to watch adults doing everyday tasks."

At least he was doing something right. "That's how I learned everything I know around here. My dad and grandfather took us everywhere they went."

"You and your four brothers?" Jade's eyes grew wide as she questioned.

"And my cousin. Sometimes, they split us up. Lucas and Asher were hard to handle together." Aaron smiled as he thought of the trouble his brothers tended to cause.

Jade laughed. "I bet you worried your mother sick."

"We did. But we learned a lot about what to do and what not to do on the ranch. That's one reason I want Levi with me—so he knows how to be safe."

"That's a good idea." Jade clicked on her computer. "There are a few I recommend that are more nature focused. Do you want a Christian curriculum?"

Aaron nodded. "Definitely."

Jade smiled. "I'm glad to hear that. I've always used Christian curriculums. For my nieces and nephews," she added.

She turned the laptop toward him and pointed the cursor to a product on the screen. "I'm thinking this one." She moved the cursor. "Or this one."

She told him about the focus units of each and what she liked about them. She was patient and thorough as she explained the importance of choosing a curriculum that fit the child's learning style.

"After I spend a few days with Levi, I'll be able to make a better decision about which I would recommend."

Aaron linked his fingers together and propped his elbows on his knees. "Thanks for going over this with me. I don't really know what I'm doing."

Jade gave him a sure smile. "That's okay. I'll just tell you what I know, and you can make a decision from there."

She could have looked down on him. She could have written him off as stupid like so many had done throughout his life. He'd struggled enough in school to know he didn't want that for Levi.

He looked at the scrapes on his worn hands. He loved having Levi by his side every day, but did he want this life for his son? Aaron was happy carrying on the family legacy, but ranching was backbreaking, non-stop, and hard on a man's body. If he gave his son the opportunity to work smarter not harder, could he spare his son years of hard labor?

Jade seemed like she was going to be a good teacher. He'd just seen her in action, and she'd have the same patience and temperament with Levi. This was the right decision, and he knew Jade was the right person for the job.

Chapter Three

JADE

"You can ride with me if you want," Aaron said as they walked out of the cabin—the cute little cabin that was her new home.

"That would be great." She wanted to admire the beauty of the landscape a little more.

Aaron walked to the passenger side of his truck and opened the door for her. While the outside was worn and dirty, the inside was quite clean. She slid into the seat and wiggled as she got comfortable. There was so much to see here, and she couldn't wait to go exploring with Levi. He probably knew all the most interesting places.

When Aaron settled into the driver's seat, she asked, "When do you want Levi's semester to begin?"

Aaron shrugged. "I'll leave that up to you. We don't have anything going on other than regular ranch duties, so there's nothing to plan around. I assumed he would start when the public schools do."

"We can do that. I'd love to have a few days to just observe him and get to know him before we settle on a curriculum."

Was she being too forward? She'd made it sound as if she and Aaron would make the decision *together*. The word *we* reminded her of team sports and families. This wasn't a baseball game, and she wasn't a part of the family.

Although, she'd love to get drafted to Team Harding. Everything around here seemed like a collective effort.

Was it wrong that she was excited to be part of the ranch dynamic?

After Aaron confessed that he didn't know much about homeschooling, she'd gotten swept up in the excitement of talking about what she loved and forgot all about her teensy crush on the cute cowboy sitting beside her.

Cute was an understatement, but she was trying to convince herself that she was overreacting to Aaron's rugged good looks.

When Aaron parked in front of the main house, he killed the engine and turned to her.

If she'd been telling herself Aaron wasn't really that handsome, her heart hadn't gotten the memo. It was currently racing in the Kentucky Derby.

"You can start whenever you're ready. I'll leave those decisions up to you."

Oh, and he had enough confidence in her on her first day to allow her to make important decisions about his son's education. No pressure.

"Okay." The word squeaked out as if she'd sucked in helium.

Aaron rested his wrist on the steering wheel and looked at the main house. "Meals are usually pretty loud, so no one will expect you to remember their names today. There are a few guests here, and they come and go every week."

Jade felt the muscles in her cheeks quiver as she strained to hold in her nervous smile.

"What I'm saying is, just relax. Supper is like throwing you into the deep end, but you'll get to know everyone soon. Most of us are family, and that's how it is around here."

How cute was that? A handsome man putting an emphasis on family.

Hush. He's not available, Jade told herself.

What if he is available? Where is his wife?

Oh, those were good questions—ones she might need to know.

Aaron turned to her with a grin that pulled to one side. "Stay close, and I'll answer any questions." He pointed to a vehicle parked nearby. "Never mind, Levi is back. You might not have time to ask questions."

That she could handle. Levi was the only thing about this new job that didn't make her nervous.

Jade met Aaron in front of the truck and followed him inside. The big meeting room was bustling with people and overlapping conversations. Her shoulders began to tense and turn forward as nervousness crept in.

Nope. I'm not going to get squirrelly. I can do this.

Teaching Levi was her job. Her performance wasn't being evaluated on factors like making a good impression with her employer's family.

Wait, she probably *was* being evaluated in that context. If the people who lived here didn't like her, Aaron might think she was more trouble than she was worth.

Aaron introduced Jade to the first person they encountered, and she stretched her smile to a laughable width.

"I'm Micah, and this is my fiancée, Laney."

"Hi!" Jade stuck her hand out with a little too much enthusiasm.

Laney gave a friendly smile. "We met already."

Get it together, Jade. You can do this. Everyone is nice here.

Laney was already stepping away as she said, "I have to grab a few more things from the kitchen, but we'll catch up later."

Micah nodded a farewell as he followed Laney.

The next closest person was a tall, intimidating man who lacked the welcoming disposition of the others she'd met.

Aaron stepped close to her until his arm brushed against hers. "Jade, this is my cousin Hunter Harding."

And when Hunter turned to her, she realized why. Did Aaron expect her to be shocked by the long scar that slid down the side of Hunter's face?

She stuck out her hand, but she had a hard time meeting Hunter's gaze. It wasn't his scar that had her tucking her chin. It was the fearsome glare he wore as he looked down at her.

He firmly gripped her hand and released it quickly. There was no "Nice to meet you," or "Welcome to the ranch" that she'd received from everyone else. Instead, she'd found herself releasing a tense breath as he excused himself without so much as a backward glance.

Just as she was regaining her resting heart rate, Aaron leaned in close, sending her back into a tizzy.

"Hunter is harmless," he whispered. "He isn't friendly either, so don't take it personally if he doesn't say much."

Jade wasn't thinking about Hunter anymore. Instead, her thoughts were bumping around like a pinball in her head as Aaron's warm breath fanned her ear.

She was in trouble—so much trouble—if she couldn't get a handle on the butterflies that swarmed whenever she thought about Aaron.

He's your boss! Shut it down! her thoughts screamed.

"Daddy!"

Jade's strained cheeks relaxed as her nervousness gave way to true joy when Levi ran from the kitchen straight into Aaron's open arms.

"Hey, buddy." Aaron squeezed his son. "Did you have fun at the Lawrences'?"

"Olivia let me pick eggs. I got lots of colors," Levi said.

Aaron set Levi back on his feet. "That's my boy."

Levi looked up at Jade. "Will you sit by me?"

The boy sure knew how to tug on her heartstrings. "Of course. We'll be spending a lot of time together, and I can't wait to get to know you."

"Dad said you're my teacher."

"He's right. I have a lot of fun things for us to do."

Levi squinted one eye, and the expression had Jade fighting a grin.

"What kind of fun things?" he asked skeptically.

"You'll have to wait and see," she said with a wink.

Levi's eyes widened. "How'd you do that?"

"What? Wink?" she asked.

"Yeah."

She winked one eye and then the other. "You mean your dad hasn't taught you how to wink?"

Levi looked at Aaron and stuck his hands on his hips. "Dad, you didn't teach me how to do that."

Aaron turned to Jade. "I don't know how to wink either. Maybe you could teach us both."

Oh no. This was some kind of test, and she was probably going to fail. "Um, I think I can manage that."

Levi held up a finger and added, "I want to whistle too!"

Jade whistled low. "I can teach you that too. Any other requests?"

Levi's brows furrowed in his concentration. "That's all for now. I'll let you know if I think of anything else."

Jade chuckled. If he thought he was running the show, he might be more inclined to pay attention to her other lessons as well.

Anita, or Mama Harding as Aaron had said everyone called her, raised her hand. "Line up! Guests first!"

Levi grabbed Jade's hand, and she fell into step behind him as he dragged her toward the huge counter filled with food.

"This smells amazing," Jade said as they stepped into line.

"It's my favorite," Levi said.

Aaron huffed. "You say that every day."

Levi grabbed a plate and shrugged his little shoulders. "I can have more than one favorite."

Aaron opened his mouth to say something, then shut it. They could correct Levi, but it wasn't a bad thing that he enjoyed multiple foods.

Jade followed Levi to the long table where he instructed her to sit in the seat beside his. She watched as the little boy put his plate on the table then tucked his hands under his thighs.

"We have to wait for the blessing."

Jade folded her hands in her lap. "Thanks for letting me know. I usually pray before eating, too."

"Papa prays for us," Levi said.

Jade looked up as a man she hadn't officially been introduced to placed his plate in front of the seat next to Mama Harding's. Everyone bowed their heads, and the room fell silent.

"Father, we thank You for the plenty You've blessed us with. We pray for our friends who are visiting and those who have come and gone. We pray for the coming work season that You would bless the work of our hands and give us strength to carry on. Please bless this food to the nourishment of our bodies and our bodies to Your service. In Jesus' name we pray. Amen."

As soon as the prayer ended, Levi's head popped up. "I'm hungry!"

Camille chuckled across the table. "When are you not hungry? You're a bottomless pit."

Levi finished chewing the hunk of meatloaf he'd shoved into his mouth. "I don't know what that is."

"She means you eat a lot," Aaron explained.

"I do," Levi confirmed. "It's because food makes me grow, and I'm gonna be as big as Daddy one day."

Jade glanced over Levi's head at Aaron. Did all little boys look up to their dads the way Levi did? She only had a sister, and she'd always thought she loved her parents equally. Did Levi admire his mother as much as Aaron?

It had been hours since Jade arrived, and it was well past the usual 5:00 quitting time. If Levi's mom worked outside the ranch, wouldn't she be home by now?

Jade pushed her wonderings aside as she tasted the first bite of the mashed potatoes on her plate. She hummed in contentment. "This is delicious."

"Yeah, Mama Harding is a master chef," Camille explained. "She keeps us all well fed."

"I love cooking," Jade said.

"What's your favorite food?" Levi asked.

Jade snuck a glance at Aaron on the other side of Levi. He was looking at her, too.

Focusing on Levi's question, she tapped her chin with her index finger. "I think my favorite is cullen skink."

"Cullen stink?" Levi asked as he scrunched up his nose in disgust.

"No, cullen skink," Jade pronounced slower. "My dad taught me how to make it when I was young. He grew up in Scotland, and it's a common soup there."

"What's in it? And what is Scotland?"

"Cullen skink is a creamy white fish and potato soup. Scotland is a country in Europe."

"Fish and potato?" Levi asked with a grimace. "Mama Harding never puts fish in her soup."

Jade laughed at Levi's candor and looked at Aaron who was also stifling a laugh. He was even more handsome when he smiled.

"It doesn't have a strong fish taste if you cook it correctly," Jade said.

Levi forked another bite of meatloaf. "Okay, where's Europe?"

"It's a long way away." She'd never finish her food if Levi kept asking questions, but she was enjoying getting to know him.

"But you said your dad came from there," Levi reminded her.

"He did. My mom and dad met there, but they came here to get married and live."

Levi's eyebrow raised. "So, your daddy left his home?"

Jade didn't miss the unease in Levi's question. Since Blackwater was his home, of course he would have a hard time understanding leaving the place where he was born. "It's okay. He wanted to go with my mom. And we travel there to see our family every year. Did you know I'm a citizen of the United States *and* Scotland?"

"What does that mean?" Levi asked around a mouthful of meat.

"It means I have two homes."

"Which do you like better?" Levi immediately asked.

Jade glanced around the table where a handful of people were listening to her conversation with Levi. Aaron was watching her too, waiting for her answer.

"I love them both. I've lived here most of my life, but I've always dreamed of teaching primary school in Scotland. Most of their schools are smaller, and they sometimes need teachers who are willing to move to the small towns to teach the children."

Levi was barely eating now. "Are you going to go teach them? I thought you were *my* teacher!"

"I am," Jade assured him. "Right now they aren't looking for teachers, and I haven't been offered a job. So, looks like you're stuck with me."

Aaron's brother, Lucas, cleared his throat across the table. "That sounds cool. Would you really go if they needed a teacher?" His gaze darted to Aaron.

Jade looked over Levi's head at Aaron who seemed to be interested in the plate he'd cleared of food. "I'd love to, but I haven't been chosen for any positions yet."

She waited a few more seconds, but Aaron didn't look at her. Had she said something wrong? He'd seemed to be enjoying the conversation as much as Levi only moments ago.

As soon as Levi was finished with his food, he started to stand.

"Nope," Aaron said, catching his son by the back of his shirt as he started to run. "Take your plate."

Levi turned around and grabbed the plate from the table before jogging across the room. Thankfully, it was nearly empty. The kid bumped and jostled the plate all the way to the end of the serving counter where a few other dirty plates were stacked.

Jade started to stand, but Aaron laid a warm hand on her shoulder.

"I'll get him. Finish your dinner. You're not on the clock when I'm around."

His kindness should be comforting. Shouldn't it? Why did his tone seem flatter than earlier? Unease settled on her shoulders. He was probably just tired. He might have been up since dawn for all she knew.

Maybe this day of firsts was just as overwhelming for him as it was for her. Finished with her own meal and tired from the long drive, Jade stood and followed Aaron.

At the serving counter, he placed his plate on the stack and turned to take hers. "You look tired. You want me to take you to your cabin?"

Jade slipped her hands into her back pockets. "I'd like that. I still need to unpack." She'd also be making notes and ordering some activity sets for Levi, but Aaron didn't need to know she browsed homeschool sites for fun.

Aaron corralled Levi and they made a few more introductions on the way out. It was still daylight outside, but her body hadn't gotten the memo. It felt as if it should be midnight.

Levi was winding down too as he climbed into the middle seat of Aaron's truck. Jade sat on the passenger seat and watched Aaron starting the truck. He hadn't so much as glanced her way since dinner.

The emotional toil of the day weighed heavy on her as she leaned against the door. Adrenaline had been running through her body like a steam engine all day. Maybe the second wind would come in handy, since she still had a few hours of unpacking to do.

As Aaron parked his truck in front of her cabin, she blinked rapidly to spark some last bit of energy.

Aaron rubbed the short scruff on his jaw. "We usually eat breakfast around daylight, but Mama does a second breakfast for guests who don't want to wake up that early."

"I can eat the early breakfast," she said. Though it would mean skipping the unpacking and going straight to bed.

"Okay. We'll pick you up at six in the morning." Aaron looked everywhere but at her as he spoke. "I guess I should show you around tomorrow if that's okay with you."

"That sounds perfect." Jade turned to Levi who had slumped against his dad's shoulder. "I can't wait to see more of the place."

Levi lazily waved. "Good night."

"Good night," Jade echoed. She looked up at Aaron who was too focused on the gear shifter to notice her. "See you in the morning."

She slipped out of the truck and breathed a sigh of relief. Her first day had been exciting and emotionally chaotic. Her emotions had rocked back and forth like the pendulum of an old grandfather clock. The changes were dizzying.

When her hand rested on the doorknob, she turned around to see Aaron watching her over the steering wheel of the truck. He seemed to have gotten over his avoidance spell because his gaze was aimed at her, intense and knowing as if he could read her thoughts.

She released a slow breath and prayed for peace. Aaron and Levi would be picking her up first thing in the morning, and she'd have a long day to spend with both of them.

She slipped inside and didn't hear his truck rev and back out until the door was completely closed.

Chapter Four

AARON

"Come on. Jade is waiting on us." Aaron buttoned his shirt as he stepped out of his bedroom.

Strangely enough, Levi was waiting by the front door. "Ready." He opened the door and sprinted off the porch.

At least someone was ready to see Jade. Aaron couldn't decide if he was up and at 'em early this morning because he was eager to see his son's pretty blonde teacher or if he was just ready to get this day over with.

He'd considered handing the ranch tour off to one of his sisters-in-law, but then he'd have to explain why he was avoiding Jade.

Levi was already in the truck when Aaron stepped out onto the porch and shut the door behind him. When he reached the truck, his son held out his cell phone.

"You left your phone in the truck," Levi said.

Aaron hadn't left it on purpose, but it was probably a blessing in disguise. He hadn't been in the mood to talk about Jade last night, and he would bet his bottom dollar he missed a few calls from his family after they heard her conversation with Levi.

He unlocked the phone to see if he'd missed anything important.

Two texts. Not as bad as he'd feared.

Camille: She's not Christina. Give her a chance.

That message didn't require a response. He was fully aware that Jade wasn't his ex. His ex was dead, but she'd left him and Levi long before she died.

The next message didn't do anything to help his morning mood either.

Lucas: My condolences.

Aaron dropped the phone into the cup holder and started the truck.

"Can we take Jade to Bluestone Creek today?" Levi asked.

Aaron shifted into reverse and glanced over his shoulder. "I think we can make it to the creek today."

"Yes!" Levi bounced in his seat.

"I'll let her know where it's safe for the two of you to play, but you know the rules too. If she doesn't know, it's your job to speak up. She's new here, and she might need some help."

"Yes, sir." Levi sat straight in the seat, ready to bound out and knock on Jade's door.

"I'm proud of you. Jade has a lot to teach you, but I know you can handle it."

Levi nodded once, firm and understanding. "I'll be sure to remember all the stuff she teaches me so I can teach you about it later."

Aaron couldn't hate that plan. "Good. I could use a lesson every now and then." He just hoped today wasn't a lesson in leavin'. Jade had sounded so hopeful last night when she talked about teaching in Scotland. He had no doubt she'd pack up and move out on a dime if she got one of those jobs.

He parked in front of Jade's cabin, and Levi jumped out of the truck. She was stepping out onto the porch and closing the door behind her before Aaron's feet hit the dirt. He'd spent most of the night blocking images of her from his mind, but she was hard to ignore standing in front of him. No matter how many times he told himself she wasn't *that* pretty, it still wouldn't be the truth. Jade was the kind of gorgeous that had her sweet smile and blue eyes seared into his mind.

Heaven help him, he was in trouble.

"Good morning! Are you ready for an adventure?" Jade asked Levi. She was incredibly peppy for the early-morning hour.

"You bet. Dad said we could go to the creek today." Levi grabbed Jade's hand and began tugging her toward the truck.

"I said we might be able to make it. I didn't say we would," Aaron clarified.

Without so much as a glance, Levi was jumping into the truck and crawling into the middle of the bench seat.

Aaron returned to the seat he'd just vacated as Jade climbed in on the other side. "Sorry, he beat me to the punch. He's a lot faster than I am."

Jade's morning smile was even more enticing than the one she'd worn yesterday. "Not a problem at all. I'm glad you're excited," she said to Levi. "I can't wait to see more of the ranch. I hardly slept a wink last night."

Aaron eyed her skeptically as he shifted into reverse. Jade was the vision of well rested. There were no dark shadows under her wide eyes, her blonde hair hung in strands of waves, and he was pretty sure she was wearing a little more makeup than yesterday.

Levi carried the conversation on the short drive to the main house, and he continued to hold Jade's attention until they stepped into the meeting room.

There were a few people Jade hadn't been introduced to yesterday, so when Aaron saw his sister-in-law, Haley, emerge from the kitchen, he led Jade that way.

Aaron began, "Jade, this is—"

"Haley Harding," his sister-in-law finished. "I've heard all about you. I don't know how I missed you yesterday." She wrapped Jade in a full-on hug.

"It's nice to meet you," Jade replied.

When Haley released Jade from the greeting embrace, they were both grinning from ear-to-ear.

"I'm so glad we have another woman on the ranch," Haley said. "Our plans to outnumber the men are coming along nicely. Let me introduce you to everyone." Haley took Jade's hand and gestured to the half a dozen people milling around before breakfast.

"That would be great," Jade said before turning to Aaron, waiting for his permission.

Aaron tipped his chin toward the waiting crowd. "Go ahead. Haley knows everyone. We'll catch up again after breakfast."

Jade followed Haley with a smile, and Levi disappeared into the kitchen. That left Aaron to catch up with Micah about any tasks that needed to be taken care of after he gave Jade the ranch tour.

All throughout breakfast, Aaron watched Jade. She could give Levi's energy level a run for its money. It was a good thing she was wired like the Energizer bunny. She was going to need it to keep up with Levi.

Aaron was finally able to relax as they ate breakfast. He wasn't expected to say much. Levi and Haley carried the conversation most mornings. Everyone else needed coffee and protein before the first order of business: the morning meeting.

When the plates were empty, Micah pulled a small notepad from his back pocket and poised a pen above it, using it as a pointer to scan the list before delegating tasks.

Aaron cleared his throat to get Jade's attention on the other side of Levi. Her chin lifted to him, and the intensity of her hazy blue eyes caught him off guard yet again.

He jerked his head toward the door, and she and Levi followed him with their plates to the serving counter.

After leaving their dirty dishes, Aaron said, "We need to get on our way if we're planning to make it to the creek today."

Jade nodded while Levi punched the air.

Aaron stuck his head into the kitchen, and Laney handed him a bag of sandwiches he'd asked her to pack for their lunch. The best part of Bluestone Creek was a good haul from the main house, and they couldn't turn around to come back for lunch.

Spending the day with Jade within arm's reach was a mental juggling act. If she kept talking to Levi, Aaron didn't have to worry about making a fool of himself. Each time Levi went off into one of his explanations about cattle feed or hay baling, Aaron struggled to pay attention and keep from daydreaming about the perfect day he was having with his son and a woman who was ten times out of his league and off-limits.

Every time he thought about the way she'd told them about her dream job, the strangling truth had him crashing back to reality. He'd failed to clarify any long-term commitment to this job, perfectly setting himself up to welcome another runner into his life.

They reached Bluestone Creek a little later than Aaron had expected, but he'd spent the morning watching Jade's amazement as they explored the ranch. He couldn't rush her. Plus, Levi had run wild at every stop they made, and he let the kid have some fun. So what if he noticed that Jade's smile widened every time Levi smiled?

Levi scooted to the edge of the bench seat as they neared Bluestone Creek on the western side of the ranch. He pointed a finger straight ahead and said, "There it is!"

Jade leaned closer to Levi. "Wow. It's beautiful."

Aaron parked the truck a few yards from the bank, and Levi bounced impatiently, waiting for someone to let him out of the middle seat. Aaron stepped out first, and Levi tore off toward the creek.

"Don't get close to the water!" Aaron shouted at Levi's back.

Jade chuckled. "Did you know that kids don't hear the 'don't' if you begin a sentence that way?"

"What?" He turned to Jade as they met up in front of the truck and followed Levi.

"If you start a sentence with the word 'don't,' children only hear what comes after it. It's like it takes their mind that first second to catch up, and the first word is lost. It's tough, but if you could train yourself to rearrange your sentences, he'll understand your command better."

Aaron looked at her as if she were a complicated puzzle with too many pieces. "I'm not sure I heard anything you just said."

She laughed, seemingly unoffended by his ignorance. "If you say, 'Stay away from the water,' he'll be more likely to understand and process what you're telling him to do."

School was in session, and Jade had just handed him his first lesson. "How do you know that?"

"I work with kids. I study their learning habits. Each child is different, and it's my job to make sure I know the best way to teach them."

Levi reached the creek and turned to run west along the bank. Aaron watched him as he thought about Jade's dedication to her work. There were so many things about raising a kid that he didn't know.

"You like teaching." It was more of a statement than a question.

Jade lifted a hand to shade her eyes from the setting sun as she watched Levi. "I do. It's never boring."

Aaron huffed. "I can imagine. Levi is a handful. Good luck getting him to sit still for a lesson."

"Well, he may just be an active learner. Some people benefit from a hands-on teaching style."

"He'll like that. That's one of the reasons I decided to homeschool. He asked a lot of questions about school in the last year, and being inside all day was his least favorite part."

"It's not a bad thing that he's active," Jade said.

Aaron watched his son stop and pick something up, his full attention on the ground as he walked. "I just don't have what it takes to do it myself." He sighed and adjusted his hat on his head. "I think Levi is smart, but he didn't get that from me."

Jade kicked a stone and cleared her throat. "Um, can I ask about Levi's mom? It's fine if you don't want to tell me, of course. I'm just curious. I haven't seen her."

Aaron hung his head. He'd known this was coming, but it hit him like a wrecking ball every time. "She died a few years ago."

Jade gasped as her hand flew to her mouth. "I'm so sorry."

Aaron stopped walking when Jade did. What else could he say? He'd never been good at saying the right words at the right time.

"Does he remember her?" Jade asked.

Aaron shook his head. "No. She left us when Levi was almost a year old. He doesn't know anything about her."

Jade's eyes widened. "Has he ever asked?"

Watching his son collecting rocks on the creek bank, the weight of raising his son alone came to a head. "No."

"Never? Not once?"

Aaron turned back to Jade. "He hasn't. I don't know why."

Jade studied Levi hopping from one foot to the other over rocks. "I wasn't prepared for this."

"Welcome to the club. Being a single parent wasn't a part of my life plan." Every part of his relationship with Christina had been unexpected. Life and the series of blows they'd been dealt had seemed unfair. Would things have been different if she hadn't been so sad? Could they have made it work? Would she still be alive if he'd been a better husband?

Funny, Aaron had been the first of his brothers to get married, but he was the one left without a wife. Life was a cruel joke. Everyone else at the ranch was happy, and he was left wondering how he'd gone so wrong and how much of his mistakes would affect his son.

Turns out the life he thought he wanted wasn't meant for him.

Jade jerked her attention to Aaron. "You seem to be handling it well. Levi is happy, smart, and confident." She shrugged and tucked her hands into her back pockets. "Your whole family is here, and I get the impression that they all help out with Levi."

"They do. I couldn't do this without them." When Christina left, he hadn't known which way was up much less how to be a single parent with a full-time job.

Jade's eyes narrowed and her mouth tugged out at the edges. It was the same expression Aaron had gotten from everyone he'd met over the last four years.

"Levi is doing fine." Jade reached out and touched his arm.

The gesture wasn't new. It was something people did when they pitied him.

But when Jade touched him, his breathing stopped. Mid-breath, everything halted. He didn't need to breathe. He needed her to stay exactly where she was right now.

Two shallow creases appeared between her brows. He focused on the blue of her eyes while he waited for his lungs to start working again.

"This explains a lot," she whispered. "That's why you were upset last night."

And what was left of his last breath rushed out, leaving him empty and cold.

"When I said I wanted to teach in Scotland. You must have thought I didn't intend to stay here very long."

He inhaled and filled his burning lungs with air, but it didn't stop the crushing weight he felt in his chest.

Yes, hearing her talk about packing up at the first sign of a job opening sounded like a replay. Except Christina hadn't given him a heads up.

It wasn't the same. He couldn't expect Jade to skip out on her dream job just because he thought she'd be the perfect teacher and caretaker for his son. That was selfish, and he'd learned a long time ago that it was stupid to think anything in life was permanent.

Her hand fell from his arm. "I'm sorry."

Aaron shook his head, ready to forget about this whole conversation. "It's okay. I understand."

He didn't. He couldn't. But he'd work on it.

Chapter Five

JADE

Jade watched as Aaron's usually stoic expression hardened further. What an extreme burden he carried. She still had so many questions but couldn't bring herself to press him further.

A knowing silence settled around them as they watched Levi high stepping through the tall grass toward them. When Jade snuck a glance at Aaron, the look of pride on his face made sense. That kid was the spitting image of his father, and the man standing beside her seemed like a good role model.

Of course, curiosity killed the cat, or in this case, curiosity killed her certainty. How could Levi's mother have left them? Had Aaron done something unforgivable? That still didn't explain why she would leave her son. It all seemed so unreal.

Levi stopped in front of Jade and Aaron with an uninhibited smile on his face. "I brought you something." He shoved both hands toward her. One held a small bouquet of wildflowers and one held a smooth, flat river rock that fit perfectly in the palm of his hand.

Jade accepted the gifts, holding them tight. "Thank you. They're beautiful."

Levi pointed at the flowers. "Those are for now." He pointed at the rock. "That's for later because flowers die."

An emotional lump caught in Jade's throat as she wrapped her hand around the rock. "I'll be sure to keep this someplace special."

Levi turned to his dad. "Can we jump in the creek?"

Aaron scoffed and crossed his arms over his chest. "That's a definite no."

"Aww," Levi groaned.

"Your dad's right," Jade said. "Let's don't and say we did."

Levi's left brow raised, forming the cutest confused expression. "What does that mean?"

"It means you'd make a good icicle, but I'd look like an ice cube," Aaron said.

Jade fought to contain the chuckle that threatened to escape. "He's right. That's not cute."

Aaron extended his hand for Levi to take. "Let's head home. It's getting dark."

"Aw, man. I'm gonna swim in that water one day," Levi moaned.

"Levi Garrett Harding, you're a mess." Jade playfully rumpled the kid's hair.

"That's not my middle name!" Levi exclaimed.

Jade shrugged. "It was worth a shot. I'll get it right next time."

Levi turned to his dad, laughing at Jade's purposeful mix-up.

She matched Levi's quick step and Aaron's long strides as they walked back to the truck while a tropical storm swirled in her middle, twisting her insides into knots.

Darkness covered the ranch before they got back to the main house. Levi had scarfed down a peanut butter sandwich before curling up to Aaron's side and falling asleep on the way back.

Just as the main house came into view over the last rise, Aaron whispered, "You want me to drop you off at the main house? Laney can fix you something to eat."

Jade shook her head, then remembered it was dark and he couldn't see her. "I'm fine. The sandwich was enough for me." Truly, the only thing the bread and peanut butter had done was riot inside her. Maybe she was getting sick.

Aaron parked the truck in front of Jade's cabin, and she stared out the windshield at her new home illuminated by the headlights.

"Thanks for today," she whispered.

"You're welcome." Aaron looked down at his son sleeping peacefully. "Thanks for taking this job. I realize you might not have expected all this. There aren't any set hours, and things will be different every day, but I—" He took a deep breath and looked up at her. "I really appreciate it."

His gratefulness was more than she could stand as guilt wrapped around her. Could she really leave him and this place if she were ever chosen for the job she'd wanted her whole life? "I'll see you in the morning."

She didn't wait for him to say good-bye as she jumped from the truck and closed the door as softly as the old metal would allow. Making a beeline for the cabin, she skipped up the steps and burst through the door, quickly closing it behind her and leaning against the cold wood.

What had she gotten herself into? She'd worked with kids for years, and she'd never felt in danger of growing too close. There had always been a special student-teacher bond, but never like this.

And never had she been so emotionally confused about a man in her life.

She'd survived her second day with Aaron and Levi, but everything inside her screamed to tread lightly. How easy would it be to keep a professional distance from Aaron and Levi? How difficult would it be to keep her heart out of the mix?

Jade pushed off the door and quickly moved to the small picture window above the kitchen sink, stepping around a few half-unpacked boxes on the way.

She watched through the window as Aaron carried Levi from the truck to the cabin like the kid didn't weigh fifty pounds.

Why did doubts invade her thoughts when she watched Aaron and his son? She felt like an intruder. They had this sweet, perfect father-son thing going on, and where did she fit into the picture?

A teacher. She was Levi's teacher and caretaker. That was all. Aaron was her boss, not her friend. She needed to set some boundaries, but how well would they hold up? She'd spent the day with them, and her emotions were all tangled up when they shouldn't be.

Jade turned from the window as Aaron and Levi disappeared into their cabin. Pulling her cell from her pocket, she called her sister, Kate.

"Hello."

"Kate, are you busy?"

"No, the kids are asleep, and I'm just cleaning the kitchen. What's up?"

Jade fought the urge to peek through the window again. "I'm in trouble."

"What? Where are you? I'll be right there. Let me just tell Ridge where I'm going."

"No, no," Jade said. "I'm really fine. I mean I'm in an emotional pickle."

"Oh." Kate seemed to deflate. "That's a relief. I never have to worry about you, so I thought the worst."

Jade sighed and squeezed her eyes closed. "I started my new job today."

"Oh, yeah. I'm sorry I haven't called to see how it's going. It just slipped my mind."

"It's fine. You have a house full of kids to keep alive." Jade loved her nieces and nephews, but they were full speed twenty-four-seven.

"Okay. I'm sitting down now. Tell me about it."

Jade looked to the ceiling of her new home as if the answer might be written in the waves and knots of the old wood. "Well, the boy, Levi, is the sweetest."

"You say that about all kids," Kate pointed out.

"I know, but he didn't treat me like a stranger. Not even for a second. The first thing he did was compliment me."

"Aww. That's adorable."

"Right? He gets his sweetness from his dad."

"Um, things just got weird," Kate tentatively said.

"Yep. Things just got weird. His dad—my boss—is incredibly handsome. Not to mention he's gone out of his way to make me feel welcome here. He and Levi showed me around the ranch all day."

The silence on the other end of the line had Jade's heart rate skipping up. "Kate?"

"I'm here. I just don't know what to say."

"Say I'm crazy."

"You're not *crazy*. Unless he's married. Then you're crazy."

"He's not married. That's the other part. Levi's mom died."

Kate gasped. "Poor thing."

"Yeah. I haven't spent enough time with him yet to know how this affects him emotionally."

"The dad or the kid?" Kate asked.

Jade let her head fall back in defeat. "I'm in over my head."

"Oh, come on. You're perfect for this job. You'll get your emotions sorted out. Is it that time of the month?"

Jade chuckled. "I wish I could blame it on unfiltered hormones, but I think I'm just not sure if I should stay here."

Kate's voice dropped to a whisper. "Why?"

"I don't know," Jade whispered back. "I've never worked with only one child before, and I'm seeing now that it'll be difficult to keep a professional boundary."

"With the kid or his dad?" Kate asked.

Jade threw her free hand in the air. "You're making this impossible. Maybe I should get out before I get too close."

"Hold your horses, renegade," Kate said in her assertive parental voice. "This job is perfect for you, you like the kid, you like your boss, they gave you a place to stay, and you said the pay is good. Why are you considering skipping out on this opportunity? Because you have a big heart, and you care about everyone too much?"

Jade walked slowly toward her bedroom. "I don't know." Maybe that was the problem. She didn't want to get too close now only to have to say good-bye later.

"All of this is silly. You're the one that adapts to anything. You've always been able to move someplace new and become a member of the community. This is just new. You'll get used to it."

Jade wasn't sure she would get used to keeping Aaron and Levi at arm's length, but she trusted her sister's advice. "Okay."

"This is the perfect job for you," Kate reiterated, overly emphasizing each word.

"Right now." Jade was still looking for the job or place where she'd settle down. There was always somewhere to move on to, always a new place to see.

"Oh, Jade. I hope you'll be happy."

"I am happy," Jade said.

"You're happy moving every few years? Starting over and leaving everything behind?"

"That's not fair. I don't leave *people*." She stressed the last word to make it clear that she wasn't abandoning anyone when she took a new job in a different state.

Kate sighed. "I know that. I guess I've just been holding out hope that you'll start your own family one day."

Jade fell back onto the bed. "I will. One day."

"You don't have to do that. I just know you'd be a great mom, and you'd make a wonderful wife."

"You never know. I might meet a cowboy out here," Jade said, her voice growing monotone at her attempted humor.

"I think there's a song about loving cowboys," Kate said.

"'The Cowboy Rides Away?'" Jade guessed.

"Not that one."

"'Where have all the Cowboys Gone?'"

"No."

"'Mamas Don't Let Your Babies Grow Up to be Cowboys?'"

Kate sounded troubled. "Yes, that's it. Wow. Cowboys have a reputation."

Jade laughed. It was so like Kate to worry about a fictional cowboy's lack of commitment. "I don't think these cowboys are going anywhere."

"Just do what you're good at. You know how to teach kids. Do your best and the rest will fall into place."

Jade bit at her thumbnail and stared at the ceiling.

"You can do this," Kate said with all the assurance of a proud mother.

"Thanks. It's just a lot to take in on my first day."

"I have to go. Call me tomorrow and tell me about your new place. I want photos."

"Yes, ma'am," Jade replied.

"Love you."

"Love you too."

Jade ended the call and let the phone fall to the bed beside her. She was freaking out for no reason. Kate was right. Aaron and Levi were nice, and this was a great job. Jade just needed to figure out how to keep her emotions out of it.

She stayed looking at the ceiling for a minute before running her hands over her waist. She needed to get out of these jeans and into some comfy PJs.

When her hand brushed over her front pocket, she felt the lump of the rock Levi had given her by the creek. She took it out, holding it up to the lamp light to study it.

She wasn't scared because she doubted her abilities as a teacher. She wasn't scared because she was attracted to Aaron on a basic level. She was scared because a little boy was searching for someone who would stay, and her history said she wasn't the staying kind. Staying was just as scary as leaving, and asking a little boy to understand was unfair.

She'd seen Aaron's face today when he told her about Levi's mother. Aaron was just as likely to be let down as Levi. No one had mentioned an end date to this job, and maybe that was something she should have asked about sooner.

Chapter Six

JADE

Jade stopped at the entrance to the Blackwater Public Library and turned to Levi. "Remember, we're supposed to be quiet in here."

Levi nodded vigorously, a smile widening on his face.

"I can't believe you've never been to the library."

Levi held his hands out, palms up, and shrugged his shoulders. "I've been busy."

This kid. He kept her on her toes, but today was all about introducing Levi to a new place. He was in his element on the ranch, but the library was a step toward getting out of his comfort zone.

Granted, they'd been working on sticking to a structured workday. There was still plenty of time to take their lessons outside. Levi seemed to adapt well to each new topic, and if his thirst for knowledge was any indication, she had high hopes that he'd love the library.

"Come on. Let's check it out."

Levi followed her into the quiet lobby where they signed in and met the friendly woman at the counter.

"Hey, we're first-timers. I'm Jade Smith, and this is Levi Harding."

The woman looked to be around Jade's age, maybe younger, with light-brown hair that draped over her shoulder in a low ponytail. She clapped her hands together and tucked them in close to her chest. "I'm Lauren, and I've known Levi since he was in diapers. Come here." Lauren stepped around the desk and held out her arms for Levi to run into them. After releasing him, she stood and extended a hand to Jade. "It's so good to meet you. I heard Aaron hired a teacher for Levi."

"It's a pleasure to meet you too." This might be the first time running into someone who knew the Hardings, but it seemed it wouldn't be the last.

"I go to church with the Hardings, but I haven't been for the last two weeks. My aunt bought a place in Arkansas, and I flew out to help her get moved in."

"Great. I've been with them the last two weeks. That means I'll see you Sunday," Jade said. Lauren had BFF written all over her.

"Sure will." Lauren turned to Levi and waved for him to follow her. "Come on. Let me show you where we keep the fun stuff."

Levi's head swiveled from side to side as if watching a ball bounce off one wall to the other and back again. They rounded a corner to reveal the brightly colored kids' area that was decorated in huge paper-mache dinosaurs. A triceratops sat atop one shelf with its head turned toward a T-Rex two shelves over. A brontosaurus greeted visitors near the entrance.

"Cool!" Levi tore off in a full run toward the shelves.

Jade reached for his arm as he whipped past, but she wasn't quick enough. Instead, she whisper-screamed toward him. "Levi Jeremiah Harding, keep your hands to yourself."

Levi turned to her only long enough to say, "Wrong again," before setting his sights on the first dinosaur.

Lauren chuckled. "Let him go. We don't get many visitors his age. I'm so glad you brought him."

"I almost fainted when he told me he'd never been to the library," Jade said.

"Oh, it's not a big deal. Mama Harding comes to our book sale every month and buys a handful of children's books for him."

Jade watched Levi stop at the first shelf. With his finger pointed at the books, his mouth began moving, but he wasn't speaking.

"It might be tough to get him into reading. He's stuck on numbers," Jade said.

Lauren crossed her arms over her chest and observed Levi. "Is he counting the books?" she asked.

"Yep. He counts everything. I can't hate it. Math lessons have been a breeze so far."

Lauren shook her head. "He must have gotten that from his mama. Aaron only made it through high school because I did his homework."

Jade turned to Lauren with renewed interest. "You went to school with Aaron?"

"Oh, yeah. We even dated once." Lauren waved her hand in the air. "Nothing ever came of it, but he was such a good guy. I did his homework because I couldn't stand the look on his face when he worried about showing his folks a failing grade. He really tried. He's just not book smart. But he's still the first person I'd call if I needed a hand with anything."

It took every bit of Jade's willpower not to press Lauren for more information about Aaron.

Especially the part about dating. Why hadn't it worked out?

"Do you think it was because of a learning disability? Or was he just not interested in academics?" Jade asked.

"I don't think there was anything wrong. He was just more of a hands-on learner."

"Like Levi," Jade added.

"Possibly. He also wasn't a fan of sitting in a classroom. That boy squirmed in his chair all day."

Jade watched Levi as he continued counting the books. He'd made it through the first shelf. "That sounds so much like Levi."

"Levi is smart. He's in my Sunday School class at church."

"I'm so glad I ran into you today."

Lauren turned around when a gray-haired man stepped around the corner, obviously looking for a library worker. "I'd better go. I'll catch up with you later."

Jade waved farewell and joined Levi at the shelves. Not willing to interrupt his counting, she began scanning the shelves for books that might apply to any of their upcoming lessons.

She'd found three books before Levi popped up beside her. "There are so many books here!"

Jade stuck a finger up to her lips. "Shh. Inside voice, please."

Levi clenched his hands into fists and gave her a wide, closed-lip smile before saying in a quieter voice, "I love it here. I just want to stay here the whole time and never go home."

Jade chuckled and rumpled his hair. "You haven't even picked out a book yet."

He turned to scan the shelves. "I want to read them all. I bet if I read ten every day, I could read them all."

"Um, maybe." She didn't have the heart to burst his bubble. She was thankful he wanted to read ten books a day. "I found these three. Why don't you pick a few, and we'll get Ms. Lauren to assign you a library card?"

***

Jade watched as Levi moved Skittles into the circle she'd drawn. Sitting at the small kitchen table in Aaron and Levi's cabin, she waited patiently while he recounted the candies.

"Ten plus seventeen equals twenty-seven." He waggled his eyebrows, proud of himself for completing the equation immediately.

"Correct." She arranged the Skittles again and leaned back in her chair, giving Levi room to work.

She heard Aaron's truck outside the cabin just as Levi's head popped up.

"Dad's home!"

She pointed at the candy on the table. He'd almost solved the problem, and she wanted to bring his attention back to their lesson. "Finish this one, then you can eat them."

Levi bent over the table with renewed energy and shuffled the correct number of pieces into the circle. He counted them with a pointed finger before announcing, "Done!"

"Correct again," Jade said, proud of him for pushing through the lesson despite the late hour. "You can eat them now."

He stuffed a handful into his mouth and began chewing. When they heard Aaron's boots on the porch, Levi chewed faster. Jade covered her mouth, trying not to laugh at his puffed-out cheeks, but both of them burst into a fit of giggles when Aaron opened the door.

Jade covered her mouth with both hands, but it did little to stop the laughter. Trying to hold it in only made her eyes water. Levi couldn't chew the candy in his mouth while laughing.

She pointed to the trash can. "Go spit that out and try again."

Aaron looked back and forth between Jade and Levi. "What's so funny?"

Jade tried to compose herself and wiped the moisture from her eyes. "I'm not sure."

Aaron's brow inched up, questioning. How many times would she have to see that expression before it stopped making her toes tingle?

Levi returned to his seat at the table and shoved only two Skittles into his mouth this time.

"It's a little late for candy, don't you think?" Aaron asked.

Jade picked up a red Skittle, her favorite color, and gracefully launched it at Aaron's head. It bounced off his forehead, and he watched its arc as it fell to the floor.

Levi was stifling another giggle as Aaron lifted his head to Jade. "Did you just throw a Skittle at me?"

Levi's belly-laugh burst free.

Jade shrugged. She hadn't wanted to poke his eye out, but she did want him to feel a *little* sting for attempting to steal their fun. "Levi just dominated his math lesson, so I thought he deserved a treat."

Aaron turned to his son. "Dominated, huh?"

Levi raised a fist and brought it down on a pile of Skittles like a hammer. "Crushed it!"

"Whoa, buddy," Jade said, gently placing her hand over his fist. "You're not helping our case."

Levi squared his shoulders and turned to his dad. "Jade likes Skittles like I do."

Aaron leaned down and kissed his son on the top of the head. "I can see that."

When Aaron's gaze turned to her, she looked up at him and sighed. It was impossible not to have feelings for this man when he continued to show her how much he loved his son.

It was just a crush. She'd get over it, but not last week or this week. Maybe next month. She'd put it on her content calendar and make it a top priority.

But today, she melted under Aaron's gaze.

Levi popped another bite into his mouth.

Aaron's stern dad voice, the one that made her knees weak, came out just long enough to say, "That's the last one for tonight. Go get cleaned up for bed. You stink."

Levi stood and playfully said, "You smell worse," before running off to his bedroom.

Aaron splayed his hands on the table and leaned forward. After a sigh, he asked, "Did you have a good day?"

After two weeks of being around Aaron, it still caught her off guard when he asked about her day before anything else. "It was great. We went to the library. He said he'd never been."

His mouth tugged to one side. It was only a fraction of an inch, but it was enough to reveal shallow creases at the edge of his eyes. "Was that a jab at me?" he asked with a light tone that told her he hadn't taken any real offense.

"What kind of dad doesn't take his kid to the library? You're on the fast track to raising a caveman."

Levi darted from his bedroom to the bathroom with a wad of pajamas in his hands.

Aaron's eyes were tired as he leaned heavier on his hands. "Sorry about that."

"Hey," she reached over and laid her hand over his before realizing that she was crossing a physical barrier that was essential to sustain between boss and employee.

She pulled her hand back as soon as she had his attention. "You're doing a great job. He's incredibly bright."

He cared so much about his son, but he always carried a weight of sorrow. She saw it when she watched Levi.

"People have basic needs that have to be met before they can absorb new information.

Children need sleep, food, water, and love before their minds can even consider learning. You've done all of that. Now it's my turn to do my part."

Aaron shifted his weight and turned toward the door where Levi had disappeared.

"Here," Jade stood. "Have a seat while I clean this up."

Aaron straightened to his full height. He was much taller than Jade, and he might have been intimidating if she didn't know of his patience and kindness.

He brushed a pile of Skittles from the table into his hand. "Thanks, but if I sit down, I'll fall asleep."

"We missed you at supper. Want me to fix you something?" The thought of Aaron going to bed hungry nagged at her caring instincts.

"Thanks, but I'll get something after I tuck Levi in."

Jade laid her hand on his arm again. He stilled, reminding her that touching her boss was frowned upon.

She pulled her hand back. She'd have to fortify her barriers. Crossing a professional line with Aaron and Levi had been her worry from the beginning. It was too easy to forget her walls when caring about them was inevitable.

"I can handle it," Jade said as she tossed the candy and scraps of paper into the trash. "You worked all day."

"You did too," Aaron replied.

"Yeah, but I got to have fun all day. I doubt you got those grease stains on your hands doing something fun."

Aaron opened his hands and inspected the black smears on them.

Jade opened the fridge. "Wash your hands. Looks like you have turkey and ham. A sandwich okay?"

She turned when she heard Aaron shuffle behind her.

"Ham sounds good," he said as he began scrubbing his hands with the grease remover soap by the sink.

She'd just opened the jar of mayonnaise when Aaron took his seat at the table.

"What do you think about the job so far?" he asked as the legs of the chair scraped against the wooden floor.

Jade kept her attention on the sandwich in front of her as she considered her answer. It had been two weeks—a wonderful two weeks. Could she tell him how much she loved it? It was the best job ever? It didn't feel like work? She was giddy to explore the ranch with Levi every day and anxious to see Aaron's sleepy smile every morning?

Could she tell him that Levi taught her just as much as she taught him?

"I don't want to speak too soon, but I'm enjoying it. Levi is so much fun, and he's doing really well."

She peeked at Aaron over her shoulder as he leaned back in his chair, seeming satisfied with her answer.

His voice was tired and raw when he spoke. "Let me know if you need anything."

She set the sandwich in front of him as Levi burst from the bathroom.

"Clean and brushed," he said as he scurried to his bedroom.

She slid her hands into the back pockets of her jeans, dreading having to leave. The day had been perfect, just like all the other days at Blackwater. "I guess I should get to my cabin."

Aaron stood. "Thanks again."

She turned at the door and said, "You know, you don't have to thank me every day. I'm happy to be here."

His tired grin was shadowed in the dim porch light. "Good night."

"Good night."

Every evening, Aaron watched her walk all the way to her cabin. And tonight, like most nights, Dixie stood guard beside her as well.

Despite the cool night air, she could feel Aaron's warm gaze on her as she walked through the tall grass to her lonely cabin.

Chapter Seven

AARON

The next morning, Aaron woke with a renewed resolve to keep a professional distance from Jade. Hearing her say she loved the job, enjoyed hanging out with Levi, and liked living on the ranch had bumped his already growing attraction to her into overdrive.

Wasn't she everything he'd always hoped to find in a woman? Someone to love him, love his son, and feel at home here at Blackwater.

And that's when he'd pumped the brakes on all thoughts Jade. She *didn't* love him, and the buck stopped there. He'd let his imagination run wild when she'd laid her innocent hand on his arm and assured him that Levi was a smart kid.

So what if she liked it here? He'd seen the fire in her eyes that first night when she talked about teaching abroad, and he wasn't sure anything would top that dream.

Aaron stole glances at Jade and Levi as he washed his hands before breakfast. It was difficult to ignore any feelings for her when she took such good care of his son.

She might like it here now, but who was to say she wouldn't change her mind? He'd seen her resume. She hadn't kept a job for more than two years, but there weren't any gaps in her employment. Had she moved on when something better came along, or had she just gotten bored?

He dried his hands. She hadn't spent a winter in northern Wyoming yet, and that might be the ultimate test. It was isolated and often unbearably cold. He was fully prepared for her to get restless the closer they got to winter.

Even Christina had been excited to live at the ranch at one point. Before it all went south, they'd been happy.

But Jade's smile as she practiced a handshake with Levi looked nothing like Christina's reserved happiness. Jade was like an open book.

When she looked up and caught Aaron staring, he fought to remember why he'd resolved to push any desire for Jade out of his mind.

"Dad! Watch our secret handshake."

Jade crossed her arms over her chest and shook her head at Levi. "Secret. It's a secret."

"But I can show Dad. We tell each other everything," Levi said.

Jade's hands went to her hips. "You said we didn't have any secrets between us either."

"We don't. I don't have that many secrets."

Jade looked from Levi to Aaron. "Did your dad tell you what he got you for your birthday?"

Levi's brow furrowed. "No. Dad, what did you get me for my birthday?"

Aaron glared at Jade. "You couldn't let that one get away?"

She grinned as if she'd won. The line between winner and loser was blurring. He didn't mind losing so much if she smiled at him like that.

"You'll find out tonight," Aaron said as he rumpled Levi's short hair.

Levi groaned before running off to greet his uncle Lucas.

"He's excited about spending the day with you," Jade said as she watched Levi barrel into his uncle.

"I am too. I can't believe he's five years old." Where had the time gone? It had been years since an infant had woken him twice a night, but it felt like yesterday.

Jade bumped Aaron's shoulder, and he turned to her. Her eyes stole his attention every time he glanced her way. The hazy blue seemed lighter today.

She jerked her head toward the serving counter. "Let's get you two fed so you can get to work."

Aaron followed her to the growing line waiting for breakfast. "What are you going to do with your day off?"

Jade shrugged. "Haley is taking me to Cody, but we haven't really decided what we'll do when we get there."

"Ah. Girl's day. I've always wondered what women do when they have a 'girl's day.'"

Jade narrowed her eyes at him. "It's a secret."

His pulse ratcheted up, and his nostrils flared. His body had crazy reactions when she was playful, and it took everything he had not to wrap his arms around her and kiss her hard.

There wasn't anything platonic about his feelings for Jade anymore, and his intentions to keep her at a distance were fading into a fog.

Jade eagerly claimed a seat beside Levi, and they jumped into a conversation as if they were best friends. When had his son started acting like a tiny adult?

"Dad said we're replacing some broken bale feeders, working on Asher and Haley's house, and then we're going for a ride on Skittle."

Jade stopped eating and rested her fork on her plate. "Skittle? Is that a horse?"

"Yeah, Skittle is my horse."

"Let me guess. You named him?" Jade said.

"Yep. Skittles are my favorite."

Jade chuckled. "I'm so glad we agree. Skittles are the best." She reached into her jacket pocket and discreetly slipped a pack of the candy to Levi.

Levi palmed the bag, not wanting his dad to see. As if Aaron didn't know about Levi and Jade's secret Skittles. Levi had colorful stains on his hands almost every evening, reminding Aaron of the woman his son had been with all day.

Jade nudged Levi's shoulder. "You better eat fast. Your dad has almost cleaned his plate."

Levi glanced at Aaron's plate before picking up a piece of bacon. "Mmm. Processed meat."

Jade swayed and clutched her chest in a fit of giggles that had small huffs of a laugh escaping from Aaron's chest. Her happiness was infectious, and before long they'd all be drunk on giggles.

Aaron grabbed his empty plate and rumpled Levi's hair. "I'll be right back. I need to make us some sandwiches for lunch."

It was half the truth. He desperately needed to get away from Jade so he could breathe.

In the kitchen, he found Haley and Laney leaned over a notebook laid out on the counter. They both looked up as he entered.

"Am I interrupting?"

"Oh no," Haley said. "We're just brainstorming the menu for next month."

"Put some burgers on there," Aaron requested.

Laney stuck her hand on her hip. "Why? Because Jade likes them?"

"No, because I like them." He did like them, but Jade had made a fuss about the burger she'd eaten last week. She said it was the best she'd ever tasted.

"Uh-huh," Haley said. "Sure."

Aaron shook his head and turned to the pantry. What did he care if they thought he was suggesting the menu be altered for Jade? She was the newest ranch recruit, after all, and he wanted her to like it here.

"What are you looking for?" Laney asked.

"I'm taking sandwiches with us today," Aaron said as he stepped into the pantry.

"I already made them. Asher and Lucas are going with you, so I made enough for everyone."

Aaron stepped back out of the pantry. "Really? Thanks."

"Yep. Lucas beat you to the punch and requested PB&J. I hope that's okay." She pointed to a bulging bag on the counter by the refrigerator.

"Suits me just fine. Thanks for lunch." Aaron grabbed the bag and waved to his sisters-in-law as they returned their attention to the notebook.

Back in the meeting room, Levi spotted him instantly and ran over. "Let's go!"

Jade was right behind him. "Have fun."

Levi wrapped his arms around her middle and squeezed. The hug ended as quickly as it began. He straightened his spine and looked up at Jade. "We'll be back soon. Don't worry about us."

Good grief, the kid could lay on the theatrics.

Jade crossed her arms over her chest and leveled him with an equally intense stare. "I'll still miss you."

Levi, Aaron reminded himself. *She'll miss Levi. Not me.*

Levi whispered, "I'll miss you too."

Aaron patted his son on the back. "Go get your boots on."

Lucas sprinted up beside them and said, "Beat you to the door," before rushing off with Levi on his heels.

Mama Harding yelled and pointed at the troublemakers. "No running!"

Aaron risked one last glance at Jade. She looked unsure and nervous with her hands tucked into her back pockets.

"See you at supper?" he asked.

"Maybe. I think Haley wanted to take me to Barn Sour for supper."

He ignored the disappointment that swirled in his chest. He could manage a day without her. In fact, he needed some space. He could forget about his inappropriate attraction if he didn't see her three times a day.

"Have fun." Aaron waved as he followed Levi outside.

He found Levi on the porch with his hands on his hips and a triumphant smile on his face.

"Shoes tied in record time!" Levi exclaimed.

Aaron examined the laces. "Nice work. You're getting better."

Levi turned and jumped off the porch, barely clearing the three stairs. "Jade has been timing me."

Aaron had taught Levi how to tie his shoes, but it was looking like he wouldn't get the credit. "What else have the two of you been working on?"

Levi opened the truck door and climbed into the seat. "It's a lot of stuff. You wouldn't understand."

Aaron started the truck. "You're probably right."

***

"Look, Dad!" Levi yelled as he jumped from the ground onto the unfinished foundation of Asher and Haley's new home.

"Nice jump," Aaron said.

Asher stood and clipped the measuring tape to his belt. "You know, some people pay good money to join a gym that lets them jump up on a box like that. They call it a workout."

Levi tilted his head in confusion. "A workout?"

"Don't worry about it," Lucas said. "You don't need a workout."

Asher leaned against the framing boards that would one day become walls. "He's right. Stick with us and you'll never need a workout."

"Watch me again." Levi jumped back to the ground before swinging his arms and jumping with all his might back onto the foundation.

Asher pointed a thumb at Levi and turned to Aaron. "What do you feed this kid?"

"Froot Loops!" Levi shouted.

Lucas started toward the truck where their sandwiches waited. "I'm suddenly hungry."

"How many times is he going to make that jump?" Asher asked.

Aaron shook his head. "No tellin'. He has unlimited energy."

Asher rubbed his chin as he watched Levi line up for another jump. "I need to ask Haley to pick up some Froot Loops."

Levi grunted and jumped again, but his toe caught on the edge of the framing. His knees and hands hit the concrete with a slap that turned Aaron's stomach.

Levi's wail pierced the silence of the ranch, and Aaron was on his feet. After helping Levi sit back and tuck his knees up, Aaron rolled up the jeans and assessed the bloody knees.

Asher sucked in a whistling breath through his teeth. "Oh, man. You did a number on those knees, bud."

Big tears streamed down Levi's dirty face, but he was already sucking air through his nose trying to be tough. "I'm fine."

Lucas jogged toward them, slowing when he saw the injury. "Uh-oh."

Asher's eyes widened. "You think he needs a new knee?"

Lucas made a show of inspecting Levi's right knee that was bloodier than the left. "Yep. Probably need to head into town for a new one."

"What?" Levi asked.

"This one is broken. Definitely need a new one," Lucas said.

Aaron let his head fall back and looked to the sky. He should probably stop his brothers before they took it too far.

Levi tucked his knees closer. "I don't want a new one."

Lucas turned to Asher who was only feeding the beast. "We should amputate then."

"What's amputate?" Levi asked.

Aaron held up a hand to stop Lucas, but his brother spoke too quickly.

"Cut it off."

Aaron watched for Levi's reaction, but the expected screaming didn't come.

Instead, Levi lifted his chin and turned to his uncle Asher with a straight face. "I think I'll just get a new one."

Aaron turned away to hide his smile, but Lucas and Asher didn't hold back as they howled in laughter.

Asher put his hands on his knees and leaned down to Levi. "Dude, Uncle Lucas is a paramedic. He'll just fix you up and we'll get back to work."

"I'll go get the first-aid kit." Aaron made a mad dash for the truck. Levi was good at putting on a brave face, especially when his uncles were around, but the gash on his knee wasn't a joke.

When Aaron returned, Levi was sitting on the cooler, content with a popsicle in his mouth.

Lucas explained everything he intended to do, and Levi listened intently. Even a warning couldn't have prepared the kid for the burn of the antiseptic. Aaron held Levi's hand as he cried until the bandage was secured around his knee.

Lucas tore off the bandage wrap and said, "Well, I have to say you're one tough cookie."

Levi puffed out his chest. "Can I be a tough popsicle instead?"

Lucas laughed and rumpled the kid's hair. "Sure thing, bud."

When Lucas packed up the kit and Asher went back to work, Aaron squatted next to Levi.

"Hey, you okay?"

Levi nodded and kept his eyes on the floor. "I want Jade."

A slice of heat lanced Aaron's chest. Levi liked hanging out with the guys on the ranch, but Aaron sometimes forgot his son was still so young and needed a more nurturing hand.

"She's in Cody right now, but she'll be back later."

Levi nodded again, accepting the absence of the one who could make him feel better.

"Let's break for lunch. Then you can take a nap in the truck."

Levi stood with a wince and accepted Aaron's hand.

Even when Jade wasn't around, Aaron was reminded of her. He knew exactly why his son was hung up on Jade because he was too. She'd become a part of every hour of their days, and forgetting about her was impossible.

Chapter Eight

JADE

"Have you ever eaten totchos?" Jade asked.

Kate laughed on the other end of the call. "I can't say I have."

"Imagine a mound of tater tots covered in about a dozen different other awesome foods."

The high-pitched sound of a talking toy sounded on Kate's end of the line. "I'm glad you got the adventurous foodie gene. I can barely eat anything after seeing mashed baby food all day."

"Then we had cake for dessert."

Kate hummed. "You have my attention. What kind?"

"I had carrot, Haley had red velvet, and Camille had chocolate."

"I wish I could have dessert. I'm still trying to shed the baby weight," Kate said.

Jade picked up the smooth rock Levi had given her from the bedside table and rolled it in her hand. "I thought it would be lonely here, but I'm already making friends."

"It sounds like you had a great day. Why do you sound glum?" Kate asked.

"I'm not glum," Jade quipped. "I'm happy."

There was a pause before Kate admitted, "Okay. Maybe I was wrong."

Jade sighed. "I just miss them."

"Aha!" Kate exclaimed. "I knew something was wrong."

"Don't sound so happy about it."

"I'm not. Who do you miss?"

Jade rested the rock back on the bedside table. "Levi."

"You said *them*," Kate reminded Jade.

"And Aaron. I had a great day, but now I'm back in my cabin alone, and I'm wondering what they did today."

"They did cowboy stuff. You know, fixing fences and riding off into the sunset," Kate joked.

"I have the day off again tomorrow because Levi's grandmother is taking him to Cody. They spend the day together every year on his birthday."

"Aww," Kate drawled. "That's so sweet."

Jade's phone vibrated against her ear, and she pulled it away to check the caller ID. Her gloomy mood slipped away in an instant, replaced by nervous excitement. "Gotta go. He's calling me."

"Who?" Kate yelled, afraid of being cut off before getting the details.

"Aaron. Talk to you later."

Kate was still saying "Bye" when Jade disconnected the call to answer the other.

"Hello."

"Hey." Aaron's greeting was deep and hesitant. "Sorry to bother you on your day off, but Levi wanted me to ask you if you'd like to come over and see his birthday present."

"Of course. I'll bring my present too."

"You didn't have to do that."

Jade slipped her foot into a shoe near the door. "It's his birthday."

Aaron's words were unsure. "I mean... thanks."

Jade smiled as she tucked the phone between her ear and shoulder to slide one arm into a coat. "See you soon." She ended the call and grabbed the large rectangular box Camille had helped her wrap today and headed out the door.

It was unnatural how much she'd missed Aaron and Levi today. They'd only been apart for a few hours. Yet, she was sprinting off the porch and through the tall grass to their cabin.

Levi met her at the door bouncing on his toes. "Guess what I got!" When he spotted the gift under her arm, he gasped. "Is that for me?"

Jade handed it to him. "Sure is."

Levi darted around Aaron and back inside the cabin.

Aaron opened the door wide for her to enter. "Thanks again for coming."

Her attention was torn between the man beside her and the boy itching to open the present.

"Can I open it?" Levi asked.

Jade turned to Aaron.

He shrugged. "Sure."

Levi tore through the wrapping paper and lifted the box. "It's a Nerf gun."

"With a target," Jade added.

Levi looked at his dad. "Can I play now?"

"One game. Then it's bedtime."

Levi tore at the box, and Aaron pulled a knife from his pocket to cut through the tape and packaging. Jade and Levi loaded the gun with the foam bullets, and Aaron hung the colorful target on the wall.

"Okay, bud. You ready? It's you against Jade."

"Ready," Levi said, standing on the other side of the living room.

Aaron crossed his arms over his chest and grinned. "Go."

Levi focused and aimed at the target before the first orange-and-green dart sailed, landing barely an inch to the right of the bullseye.

All three of them jumped in celebration. She was so proud of his determination and precision. He was five years old, but his motor skills were still developing. Thankfully, she'd found him a gift he'd love.

After a few more rounds of target practice, Aaron clapped loudly. "Okay, kids. Time for bed."

Levi looked to her with a pitiful expression. "Do you have to go?"

"I'll see you in the morning," she assured.

"Can you tuck me in?"

Jade looked to Aaron for an answer.

Aaron shrugged. "I don't mind, if you're okay with that."

She patted his back. "Get dressed, and I'll be there in a minute."

Levi darted to his room, and she began picking up the darts.

Aaron squatted next to her to help. "Thanks again for this. He completely forgot about the present I got him."

"Oh, yeah. What was it?"

"A climbing dome like you see at playgrounds. I thought he could expel some of that endless energy."

Jade smiled. "He'll love that."

Levi jogged out of his room clad in checkered pajamas. "I'm ready." He turned to Aaron. "Night, Dad."

Aaron's jaw tensed, before he leaned to kiss his son's forehead. "Night, son."

Levi took off for his room, but Jade was watching Aaron. He tipped his head toward his son's bedroom. That might be the only go-ahead she'd get, but she was still unsure. By saying his good nights out here, it was clear Levi thought only Jade would be tucking him in. Why did it feel like she was stripping something away from Aaron?

Levi was already in the bed by the time she stepped into his room.

"What do you do before bed?" she asked.

Levi shrugged. "Not much. Dad just tells me good night and we pray."

She sat on the side of the bed. "Do you want me to pray tonight?"

"Sure."

Jade bowed her head. "Heavenly Father, thank You for the wonderful day You gave us. I pray that You continue to watch over us and guide us. Please forgive us of our sins and shortcomings, and help us to grow closer to You. In Jesus' name we pray. Amen."

"Amen," Levi said as he squirmed beneath the covers.

"Good night."

"Night, Jade. See you in the morning."

Jade brushed a hand over his soft hair before he turned on his side. She cared about him so much after only a short amount of time. He was opening her heart in ways she never thought possible, and it was difficult to walk away from him.

Aaron was waiting for her when she closed the bedroom door. He pushed his shoulder off the wall he'd been leaning against and shifted his weight from side to side.

"He did fine," she said.

"It's the first time I haven't tucked him in."

"It's not the end. It's just one night. He still needs his dad to tuck him in," she assured.

He brushed a hand down his face, and she spotted various emotions flash across his features—hurt, love, and uncertainty.

He didn't have to say it. This man loved his son whole-heartedly.

Aaron sighed, and his expression narrowed to one of contentment. He nodded toward the kitchen. "How was shopping?"

She followed him into the small kitchen where he pulled out a chair for her. "It was great. Haley is a riot."

He chuckled. "That she is. She keeps us on our toes. Coffee?"

"Do you have decaf?"

"Sorry. I only have caffeinated."

"It's fine. I can have a cup." In truth, she'd be up well into the night after drinking coffee this late, but she didn't want to miss out on the company. She wasn't ready to leave just yet.

Aaron turned away from her to start the pot. "What else did you do?"

"Camille met us at Barn Sour for dinner."

He crossed his arms over his broad chest as he leaned back against the counter. "What did you think?"

"We had a blast. I tried totchos. They're amazing, by the way. Then we lined up way too many songs on the jukebox."

Aaron's smile quirked to one side. "You danced, didn't you?"

"Guilty, and I won't apologize." She'd never been one to dance like no one was watching, but Haley and Camille hadn't given her much of a choice.

He shook his head. "I hate that I missed it."

"What about you?" she asked.

He turned to grab two mugs from the cabinet. "We helped out at Asher and Haley's place for a while, put a few bale cages together, and rode around the south pasture. "I'm still not ready to let Levi ride on his own, so we rode Skittle, and Maddie rode Dolly."

Jade had met Maddie her first day at the ranch, and they'd promised to get together on some riding lessons for Jade. She didn't have much experience with horses, and Maddie was thrilled at the idea of teaching someone new about her love of horses.

Aaron filled two cups before turning to her. "I have sugar but no creamer."

"No problem. I'll take it black."

He handed her a white ceramic mug with the scrawled letters L-E-V-I across the front. The one Aaron kept for himself read D-A-D in the same unsteady handwriting.

"Actually, our father-son day was mostly spent talking about you."

Jade wrapped her hands around the warm mug and bit her lips between her teeth. What should she say? Was a high-pitched squeal appropriate? Punch the air? Victory dance?

Excitement pushed against the walls of her chest, begging to be released.

Instead, she blew the steam that rose from her coffee and casually asked, "Really?"

Aaron nodded. "All good things, of course." He tapped the side of his mug. "He's really attached to you."

He had no idea how much it meant to her to hear him say those words. How often had she struggled to connect with a child she desperately wanted to teach? Some children were harder to understand than others, just like adults. But with Levi, everything had been simple from the beginning. She'd been able to accomplish so much in the time she hadn't needed to spend figuring out how to gain his trust and be granted access into his safe space. Levi had welcomed her in immediately.

"I'm really attached to him too." She raised the cup to her lips and swallowed the coffee along with the lump that had clogged her throat.

If she were honest, she was slowly becoming attached to Aaron too. She'd planted herself beside Levi, but the roots of her heart were reaching toward Aaron as well.

His gaze was fixed on her, observing while anchoring her attention to him. "What are your plans for tomorrow?"

"I don't really have any. I only had a few errands to run in town, and Haley helped me get those taken care of yesterday." She traced her fingertip along the lines of Levi's name on the mug. She'd put off thinking about tomorrow mostly because she wasn't looking forward to being lonely all day while Mama Harding took Levi to Cody for his birthday.

She waved a hand in the air, trying to appear unaffected. "I'll probably just browse homeschool curriculums online. I have *way* too many already, but I like looking anyway."

"No wonder you're great at your job."

Jade looked up from her coffee, and excitement grew tighter in her chest. It was a simple thing to say, but she desperately wanted to excel at her job. It was the most important thing in her life behind her faith in the Lord. Children were precious, and her passion was to nurture their curious minds.

"Thank you." The words were a whisper, but the sentiment behind them was powerful.

Aaron's gaze fell to his mug, engulfed by the strong hands that worked from sunup to sundown to keep this ranch running. "I was wondering if you'd like to hang out. Tomorrow," he added.

Her heart raced at his words, and she fought to contain her elation. She'd be doing backflips in the grass between their cabins when she left here. The coffee may have had a hand in fueling her adrenaline, too.

"Is this an evaluation?" she joked.

Aaron shrugged one shoulder. "Nah. Levi talked you up, and I'm just curious what all the fuss is about."

She leaned forward to playfully swat his arm. "Stop it. I'd love to hang out with you. I honestly have no idea what you do around here."

He raised his cup to his lips. "It's not that interesting, but I was thinking we could sneak in a horseback ride in the afternoon."

Jade clasped her hands together. "I'd love that."

They talked about Levi, and she bragged on his progress. Aaron told her about some of the funny things Levi had said, and they both tried to contain their laughter. Levi was asleep, but he'd be quick to jump out of bed if he heard them having a good time without him.

Soon, Jade's cup was empty, and Aaron stood, taking it to the sink. "It's getting late. Let me walk you home."

Walk her home? He'd always watched from his front doorway. Was she reading too much into the thirty steps between his cabin and hers?

Thirty steps felt like one big step toward a change in their relationship. Did she want that? Of course she did, but was it *right* for her to want that?

"You don't have to do that," she said while praying he didn't rescind his offer.

"I don't mind. Levi will never know I'm gone."

Aaron walked close behind her to the door where they grabbed their jackets. Despite the slight chill in the night air, she felt warmer with Aaron so close.

On the way to her cabin, Aaron walked close enough that their shoulders brushed. He scanned the moonlit ranch, ever vigilant. He was a protector by nature. It was one of the reasons he was a good father to Levi. The broad, handsome man beside her was built to be the head of a family.

He was a gentle guardian with the stature of a grizzly bear but sweet like honey.

She softly chuckled at the conjured image of grizzly bear Aaron as they stepped onto the rugged porch of her cabin.

"What's so funny?"

She turned at the door. "I just had a funny thought."

"About what?" he asked, deep and quiet, as he moved closer to her and the door at her back.

"You." The word was barely a whisper.

"I'm not sure I like the idea of you laughing when you think of me."

She stared up at him. The dim moonlight shone behind him, blanketing his face in shadow. There wasn't anything humorous about the man standing in front of her. She didn't breathe as he leaned in, his intense gaze holding hers captive.

His deep voice sent a trail of fire down her spine. "My reasons for asking you to come with me tomorrow have nothing to do with your job. I know exactly why Levi is hung up on you."

And time slowed as she let every word sink into her skin and take root. Oh, boy. She was hooked, and she didn't have the will to fight it. She wanted him to close the distance between them. If he didn't kiss her now, her heart might explode. She wasn't in danger or running a marathon, but her speedy heart hadn't gotten the memo. Aaron Harding was close enough to grab and hold onto, and that was enough to send her adrenaline into overdrive.

His breaths were deeper and quicker, signaling her own lungs to work overtime.

But instead of leaning in, his attention turned back to his cabin. A second of indecision flitted over his dark features before he turned back to her. "I should go."

She didn't move, paralyzed by the anticipation of the kiss that never transpired, as he took two laborious steps back.

"Okay." The word was hollow, but it was as much as her clouded brain could force at the moment.

"Good night."

He was off the porch and moving through the darkness with purpose before she'd recovered from the effects of his presence on her central nervous system.

"Good night." Her farewell was a whisper engulfed by the wind as she turned around and went inside.

Chapter Nine

AARON

The next morning at breakfast, Aaron chewed bacon on autopilot, spending way too much effort trying not to stare at Jade.

He was in so much trouble. He definitely hadn't been thinking clearly when he asked her to spend the day with him. No, he'd walked her to her door and leaned in like they were in high school and he was dropping her off on her parents' front porch fifteen minutes before curfew.

Jade Smith had his mind twisted up in knots. He wanted more of her.

But that was just curiosity, right? He tried to explain the allure of mystery to his knowing mind, but all evidence pointed to the truth.

Aaron was hung up on his son's nanny, and he was in trouble.

"Dad! Jade said she can teach me sign language!"

Aaron blinked hard and turned to Jade. Why didn't it surprise him that she knew sign language? Jade had sat on a ridiculously high pedestal ever since she arrived.

"That would be a great skill to learn." He hoped she taught Levi everything she knew. Maybe his son would be spared the backbreaking ranch work.

The work wasn't all bad, but he hadn't hit thirty yet, and certain parts of his body were getting ready to wear out.

Then Jade smiled at him, and he fought the urge to pull her in. It had taken every ounce of restraint not to kiss her last night. Thankfully, a fleeting thought of Levi had snapped him out of the trance he'd fallen into.

He'd been so close. The smell of her sweet shampoo had tingled in his nose, pulling him in.

He'd been so tempted, until reality hit him in the chest.

She was his son's nanny. He'd hired her in a professional capacity to take care of the one person on this earth he loved most. The last thing he wanted her to think was that she was expected to bend to his every will simply because he wrote her paycheck.

The lines were blurred, and professional and personal were already blending.

He snuck a glance at her as she explained to Levi the differences between scones and biscuits. She didn't seem nervous about spending the day with him. Did she feel forced?

After breakfast, everyone waved their good-byes to Mama Harding and Levi, who ran back to wrap his arms around Jade.

Aaron would just ask her. He could do that. They were adults. She didn't have to do anything she didn't want to.

"You ready to go?" she asked.

When she smiled and bounced on her heels like that, he could almost convince himself it wasn't necessary to ask again.

"Are you sure you want to come? I mean, you don't have to if you don't want to."

She narrowed her eyes at him. "Are you rescinding your invitation?"

He held out a hand to stop her. "No. Definitely not. I'm just not sure you're up for this. It might be boring."

"Couldn't be worse than poking around on the internet all day."

"Fair enough." He gestured for her to lead the way.

She stepped onto the porch before turning to ask, "What are we doing first?"

"I need to put Levi's birthday present together." Aaron walked to the back of his truck and let down the tailgate. He pulled the box to the end of the bed and took out his pocketknife to slit the tape. "It was his favorite for all of two seconds. You know, until you showed up with the better present."

She laughed. "I did not. This one is definitely better."

Aaron shrugged. "It's fine. The kid has dozens of things to keep him entertained around here."

Jade looked around and asked, "Where are you putting it?"

"I'm not sure yet. I was thinking over there"—he pointed to the small patch of flat ground on the right side of the main house— "or over there"—he pointed to the larger flat area on the other side.

Aaron turned to see Jade surveying the area.

"What do you think?" he asked.

"I like that side better." She pointed left. "It has more evening sun."

Aaron picked up the box and started toward the left side of the house. "We'll go with your pick."

Aaron pulled pieces from the box while Jade opened the instructions. She read, and he assembled.

When they'd finished, Aaron looked from the metal dome of geometric shapes to Jade. The ease with which they'd worked together was unexpected.

"It's awesome. Levi is going to love it." Jade bounced on the balls of her feet beside him and wrapped her hands around his arm. She radiated happiness.

Being this close to her unbridled excitement was intoxicating. He wanted to grab her and crush his mouth to hers. The muscles in his arms tensed, aching to hold her.

When she calmed beside him, her smile lingered. Was he imagining it, or were those hazy blue eyes tempting him to cross every line?

Aaron pushed out a heavy breath. "You up for feeding the cows now?"

She released his arm. "Yes. Let's do it."

They climbed back in the truck and drove to the north barn. One side was completely enclosed with three overhead doors, while the other side was a pole barn that housed equipment in the middle bay and hay in the outer bay.

Jade followed him toward the tractors as her eyes scanned everything in sight. "I barely got a look at this place when you brought me here last time."

He lifted an overturned bucket to reveal a pile of keys in a dented metal pan. He shuffled the keys until he found the one he needed. "There's not much to see."

"I respectfully disagree. You're just immune to this amazing view."

He looked out over the north pasture. The sun hung bright in the clear, blue sky, and the fence was the only man-made thing in sight.

Aaron scratched his chin. "I guess you're right."

She took a deep breath and exhaled in a rush. "This place is gorgeous. I'll never get tired of it."

Aaron turned to watch her expression. Did she really believe that, or did he want to hope it was true?

He cleared his throat and pointed to the tractor. "You want to ride with me?"

Jade looked up at the enclosed cab. "Is it safe?"

"It is. Levi rides with me all the time."

She squinted her eyes at him. "Is there enough room for both of us?"

Aaron thought of the small space, and his heart rate spiked. "Maybe. Levi's a lot smaller than you are, but I think we can squeeze in together."

The color in her cheeks bloomed pink as she chewed her bottom lip.

Aaron had no chance of denying his feelings for Jade. Not at this point. He was too far gone and practically sprinting for the cliff where he would gladly fall head over heels for this woman.

She turned to him and shrugged. "Okay. Let's try it."

"I'll get in first, and we'll fit you in."

He showed her where to step as he climbed up the side of the tractor. At the top, he turned around to offer her his hand.

Jade focused on each step as she climbed. When she reached the top, he realized how small of a space they had to squeeze into.

Her eyes darted around him. "Where do I—"

Aaron sat in the bucket seat and motioned for her to sit on his thigh. She gently sat with her legs between his knees and looked around.

"If you're not comfortable with this, you can hang out in the barn for a little bit. I can put out the bales quickly."

Jade turned to him. "I'm okay."

Her face was only inches from his. With her side nestled close against his chest, it was difficult to think clearly.

"Can you close the door?" he asked.

She reached for the handle and pulled the Plexi-glass door closed. "You're sure this is safe?"

Aaron started the engine and released the park brake. "If I wasn't confident that you were safe, I promise I wouldn't have suggested it."

Jade grinned. The rumbling of the engine almost drowned out her words. "I should have known that."

He reached around her to shift the gears, explaining each one he touched. When the tractor jerked into motion, she braced herself with one arm wrapped around his shoulder.

Raising his voice to be heard over the tractor, Aaron told her where they kept the hay, how to operate the tractor, and the most important safety measures to remember while operating the machinery. With her ear so close, he chose to lean closer instead of raising his voice to be heard above the noise.

He speared the round hay bale and turned the tractor. Pointing to the round, metal cage atop the closest rise, he told her where each bale cage was located. She watched with intense focus as he operated the controls. She asked a few questions and pointed out things she found exceptionally beautiful.

When they finished putting out the hay, he directed the tractor back toward the pole barn. He killed the engine, and silence settled around them.

Jade laughed, and Aaron drank in the sound of her joy.

"That was so much fun."

Aaron had to agree. Holding Jade close was the highlight of his day. "I'm glad you had a good time."

Jade didn't move to stand from his lap, and his hand wrapped around her waist. He wanted to pull her in, kiss her mad, and tell her how much it meant to him that she'd squeezed into the constricting cab of a tractor to be by his side today.

Her gaze dropped to his mouth, and his arms wrapped tighter around her, pulling her closer.

"Jade." He hadn't meant to whisper her name, but she filled every ounce of space inside him. She seeped into the cracks and knit the broken shards inside him until he wondered if he belonged to himself or if she had completely taken over, filling a part of him he hadn't realized was hollow until it was overflowing with the joy of Jade.

"Yes." That one word she spoke seemed to answer a question he hadn't thought to ask.

"I don't know what's happening, but I'm not supposed to care about you the way I do." His gaze fell to her lips for a moment before he averted his attention away from them. "I can't stop it."

Her chest rose and fell with deep, filling breaths. "I can't stop either." Her arms tightened around his shoulders. "I don't want to."

Aaron's lips crashed against hers, and he breathed deep, gasping for more of her. He drank her in, crushing his lips to hers, pulling her dangerously close as his embrace tightened. One hand gripped her waist while the fingers of his other hand snaked into her blonde hair.

Her mouth slid easily over his, soothing the ache she'd created inside of him. His heart beat louder and faster, calling to her in the most primal way. The rush of his tempered desire of the last few weeks crashed into her harder and more violently than the unforgiving waves of the sea in a storm.

He released her and inhaled deeply. Her eyes slowly opened, and she raised a hand to her lips.

Aaron's gaze slid over her, taking her in until his breathing calmed. Neither of them spoke, but the unspoken words swirled around them.

Had he ever been caught up in a storm of feelings like this? He recalled the love, confusion, and fear he'd felt when Levi was born. Sitting here with Jade in his arms evoked a response akin to the torrent of that day.

She was the one he hadn't known to expect. She was the one God had placed into his path to heal the wounded parts of his soul. She was the one he wanted to cherish and appreciate. Every move she made and every action she took was born of kindness.

The magnitude of the change in their relationship hit him square in the chest, demanding he acknowledge its presence.

He was falling for Jade, and he didn't want to stop it.

She rubbed a finger across his jaw. "Wow."

Contentment swelled in his chest at her satisfaction. "You said it."

"I've been thinking about that since I met you."

"Me too. You're hard to resist."

She chuckled and turned to survey the path leading down from the lofty tractor cab. "How do we get out of here?"

Aaron squeezed his arms around her for a moment before releasing her. "Very carefully. I won't let you fall."

Jade slowly descended from the cab. Aaron was close behind her, much surer of the placement of each step.

He stashed the key beneath the bucket and offered her his hand. She grabbed it and fell into step beside him on their way back to the truck.

"You up for riding today? We can stop in for lunch and still have a little bit of time before Mama and Levi get home."

"Sounds good, but I have to tell you that I've never been on a horse before."

"Really? Maybe we'll just let Maddie go over the basics today, and you can decide after that if you're ready to start today."

She released a heavy breath. "That would be great. I'm not sure what to expect, but the idea of getting on a horse feels daunting right now."

He opened the passenger truck door for her and said, "No pressure. We can take it slow."

Jade slid into the seat, and he closed the door. There were a few other things in life he might want to take slow, but it was difficult to be patient in his relationship with Jade when his feelings were so clear.

She was still his son's nanny, he was still her boss, and she might still leave if a better job offer came along. What did he have to offer her here that could be better than her life-long dream?

Neither of them spoke as they drove back to the main house for lunch, but she didn't hesitate when he reached for her hand. Her fingers slid into the spaces between his as if they completed a puzzle that had long been unfinished.

When they topped the small rise just before the main house, Jade sat up straighter. "Is that Mama Harding's car?"

"Looks like they came back early."

"I hope nothing is wrong," she said.

Aaron squeezed her hand. "Don't worry. They would have called me."

"Right." Her grip relaxed, and her smile returned.

Levi burst through the door before Aaron had parked the truck. Jade jumped out as Levi jogged toward her.

"We're back! I got a swing set!"

Levi crashed into Jade and wrapped his arms around her as Aaron stepped out of the truck. When Levi released his hug on Jade, he looked up at her with a broad smile. "Come see it!"

He ran back into the main house, tugging Jade along behind him. She turned back to Aaron with a smile to match his son's just before Levi pulled her inside the house.

Asher dodged them as they barreled through the door. "Whoa. Pardon me." He hooked a thumb over his shoulder at Jade and Levi as they ran past. "They left you out here?"

Aaron stuck his hands in his jacket pockets and slowly made his way onto the porch. "I didn't have a chance with Jade around."

Asher pushed a foot into his boot. "To be fair, she's much prettier than you."

"You're tellin' me."

"What's going on with you two anyway? Haley thinks I know something I don't, and she won't give me any peace."

Aaron shrugged and toed off his boots. "I care about her, and Levi cares about her. But she's too good for me, and she wants something I can't give her." Reality kicked him in the gut.

"Teaching in Scotland?" Asher asked.

"Yeah." The elation that had followed Aaron through the morning was overshadowed by the black cloud of reality. The kiss they'd shared earlier had been a moment of weakness. How soon would it be before she regretted it? "We shouldn't get anything started between us."

"But you're human, and it's impossible to stop caring about someone, even if you shouldn't."

"Right," Aaron said as he scratched the stubble on his jaw. "I've seen this movie before. She leaves, and I won't be the only one with a broken heart this time."

Asher clapped a heavy hand on his brother's shoulder. "If there's one thing I've learned from being married to Haley, it's that people don't always do what you expect them to do."

Aaron shook his head. "It's not fair to ask her to stay if she wants to go. If she doesn't want us enough to stay in Blackwater, then she isn't what's best for Levi and me."

"Fair enough, but things aren't always so black and white. I tried to tell myself I could let Haley go because it was the right thing to do, but I was wrong, and I couldn't stop loving her."

Aaron grabbed the doorknob. "I better get in here."

Asher rested his wide-brimmed hat on his head. "See you."

Aaron stepped inside and caught sight of Jade and Levi where they stood near the kitchen showing their latest handshake to the new couple who had checked into the bed and breakfast the day before.

Was there a reason Asher had used the same words Aaron had spoken to Jade earlier?

I couldn't stop loving her.

Aaron hadn't said he loved Jade, and maybe that was the difference. Did it change the situation if he merely couldn't stop admiring her? If he couldn't stop appreciating her? If he couldn't stop caring about her?

Levi's eyes widened when he noticed Aaron. "Dad!"

Jade was behind his son, and her expression mirrored Levi's.

How could he possibly stop the feelings that were rushing toward love if she kept looking at him like that?

Chapter Ten

JADE

Jade clutched her Bible to her chest and tried to sneak around the perimeter of the sanctuary. The pews of the small church were mostly filled, and she pushed up higher on the toes of her low-heeled shoes as she searched for the Hardings.

She'd left the ranch a few minutes after the family and gotten stopped at a railroad crossing, making her fashionably late to church. She hated being late. She'd planned for everything—except a train.

A worship song ended, and Jade spotted Haley's auburn hair a few rows ahead. With a whispered, "Hey," Haley scooted over to make room for Jade.

The music minister began a new song, and Jade inhaled a deep breath before picking up the lyrics. It was one of her favorite songs. She had many "favorite" songs, but this one always had her singing louder and freer.

She felt a tap on her shoulder and turned to see Lauren silently waving for Jade to follow.

Placing her hymnal on the pew beside her Bible, she retraced her steps from minutes before as she followed Lauren out into the hallway.

Once the door to the sanctuary closed behind them, Lauren reached for Jade's hand. "I'm sorry to pull you out of the service, but I could use your help."

"Of course," Jade said immediately. "Anything."

Relief washed over Lauren's face. "Robin and Kathy usually take turns teaching the four and five year olds in children's church, but they're both out sick. I would add them to my class, but we have a lot of kids this morning." Lauren placed her hand over her heart. "Would you mind helping me?"

Jade squeezed Lauren's hand. "I'd love to. Let's go."

"Thank you. Dorothy and Jerry Higgins are watching them now. I told them I'd rush back."

Jade followed Lauren down the hallway in a brisk walk. It had been a few months since Jade had led a Sunday School class, and she'd missed teaching a room full of kids.

Lauren opened the door to find Tim leading an animated chorus of "Joshua Fought the Battle of Jericho." Almost two dozen kids sang along, waving their hands.

Levi spotted Jade and his eyes grew wide as he made his way around the others to get to her. They'd only been apart for half an hour, but Levi barreled into her arms as if they hadn't seen each other in a month of Sundays.

"What are you doing here?" Levi asked.

Jade pulled out of the embrace. "I'm helping Ms. Lauren teach your Sunday School class today."

"Yes!" Levi bounced in delight.

"Go find your seat so we can find out what Ms. Lauren has planned for us today."

Levi hurried off to reclaim his seat as Lauren expressed her thanks to the Higginses for stepping in.

When the classroom door closed, she turned and raised her hand. "Who is ready to learn about Jonah and the whale?"

A chorus of "Me" peppered the room.

Lauren walked Jade and the students through the activities. They both moved around the room, wrangling toddlers and instructing the pre-school children.

When the twinkling of bell chimes filled the room, Jade looked for the source of the music.

"That's our cue to start tidying up. You know what to do. Cups and plates go to the trash, and all markers get matched with a cap."

Parents began showing up before they'd finished cleaning up, and they left with friendly waves, smiling children, and heartfelt thanks.

Aaron showed up with the other parents, and his eyes widened when he spotted Jade.

"I thought you left. I texted you."

Jade collected safety scissors into a clear plastic tub. "Oh, I'm sorry. I left my phone in the car. Lauren needed some help today."

Lauren stepped up beside Jade and wrapped an arm around her shoulders. "Thank you for helping. I'd have been a mess without you."

"I doubt that. You're a wonderful teacher, and the kids had a great time."

Levi ran up to Aaron and tugged on his hand. "Dad, I need to find Mama Harding and show her the card I made for her."

Aaron tipped his imaginary hat at Jade and Lauren. "See you later."

The last parent left with their child as Lauren tied up the trash bags.

"Listen, I know I kind of sprung this on you today, but I've been meaning to talk to you about children's ministry for a while now. Would you be interested in becoming a regular teacher?"

Jade was still feeling the excitement of teaching a large group of kids, and the offer felt like the answer to a prayer she hadn't thought to pray yet. Should she say yes? She wanted to. Everything inside her leaned toward accepting the offer.

But *could* she accept it? She wasn't an official member of the church yet, but moving her membership from her home church in Missouri had crossed her mind a few times since she'd been in Blackwater.

"I enjoyed being a part of your lesson today. I would love to, but I'd like to pray about it."

Lauren squeezed Jade's hand. "Yes, pray about it, and let me know if you have any questions. Here's my number."

Jade and Lauren walked out of the church together, and the parking lot was nearly empty. A few people still gathered near the entrance chatting.

Jade waved good-bye to Lauren as they parted ways. Jade's circle of friends here in Blackwater grew almost daily. She was beginning to feel like a part of this special town.

She stopped when she saw Aaron leaning against her minivan. The other Hardings had already gone.

"Hey, is everything okay?" she asked.

Aaron pushed off the door and slid his hands into his pockets. In a green-and-brown pearl snap shirt, a nice pair of dark-wash jeans, and clean boots, he looked equally dressed up and comfortable at the same time.

"Yeah. I just thought I'd wait around for you." He hooked a thumb over his shoulder. "Levi rode home with Noah and Camille."

"You didn't have to do that, but thank you anyway." She smiled and playfully pinched his cheek. "You just wanted to check out my ride, didn't you?"

Aaron cut his eyes to her tan minivan. "Yes. I've been curious about that."

She gestured to the passenger door. "You may enter the magic school bus."

Aaron chuckled. "Really?"

"Yes. You may address me as Ms. Frizzle for the remainder of this adventure."

Aaron shook his head and slid into the passenger seat with a grin.

Jade tried not to read too much into Aaron's decision to wait for her, but it felt as if the butterflies in her stomach had a six-inch wingspan and were fluttering relentlessly.

She parked beside a row of pickup trucks in front of the main house. Only a few regular ranch vehicles were missing.

Aaron met Jade in front of her minivan and reached for her hand. They hadn't talked about the kiss they'd shared yesterday, and she'd worried things would be awkward between them or he would regret his decision, either seeking her out to label it a mistake or avoiding her to make the same point.

As they ascended the steps leading onto the porch, Jade felt her phone vibrate in the small purse at her side. Using her free hand, she slipped the phone out. "This is my Gran, can I meet you inside?"

"Sure. Take your time. I'll save you a seat." Aaron kissed her forehead just below her hair line before toeing off his boots and heading inside the main house.

Gran called at least once a week and always in the afternoons. With the time change between Scotland and Wyoming, Jade's lunchtime was near Gran's suppertime.

"Hello."

"Hey," Gran answered in a lazy voice. "How was your week?"

"Wonderful." Jade sat on the top porch step and looked toward the ranch entrance. About one hundred yards away, the long dirt drive was lined with thick forest on both sides all the way to the main road that led into Blackwater.

"I got the pictures you sent. The ranch is as beautiful as you say it is."

Dixie ran toward Jade from the right side of the main house and stopped in front of her with her head tilted up, waiting for attention.

Jade scratched Dixie's white fur behind her ear. "The photos don't do it justice."

"It's good to hear you're happy where you are. You've seemed uncertain for a while now."

"I'm not uncertain," Jade said. "I just—"

She just hadn't heard from the Scottish school system about an opening. She'd applied for every job that came available, but she hadn't seen a new opening in months. That was the uncertainty she'd been carrying for years. Since she'd been at Blackwater, she'd thought about the dream job that may never come less and less.

"You like the new job?" Gran asked.

"I do. And I actually got the chance to help out in the children's church this morning."

"Oh, I bet you enjoyed it."

"I did," Jade said. "They asked me to be a regular teacher."

"That's wonderful. I know you'll do a wonderful job."

Dixie stood and moved to Jade's other side, still offering her neck for Jade's attention.

Jade directed the conversation back to her grandparents. "How is the restaurant?"

Her grandparents had owned The Four Winds, a small restaurant in Fort Augustus, for decades, and they were still a part of its day-to-day operations.

"The tourist season is ending, but business is steady."

Jade had grown up spending summers and Christmases at the family restaurant. Everyone in the area knew her grandparents, and her memories of the place and the people had her chest aching to visit home.

"You'd love Mama Harding's cooking. Everything she makes is delicious."

"I'd love to visit. You speak highly of her. If you keep sending beautiful photos, I may just book a flight soon."

As much as Jade would love for her grandparents to visit Blackwater, she knew the trip would be exhausting for them, and they didn't like leaving the restaurant for too long.

"I'll have to talk to Aaron about taking some time off to come visit."

Gran hummed. "You sure have a good boss. It's not every day you get to work with someone like that."

Jade had been telling Gran about Aaron and Levi for weeks, and she was dying to tell her about the kiss, but something held her back. She still wasn't sure what the kiss meant, and the reminder that Aaron was her boss settled like a heavy rock in her stomach.

"I know. He's a good man." She didn't hide the longing in her voice from her grandmother, but she changed the subject to avoid any more talk about Aaron. She still wasn't sure what to think about the change in their relationship lately. "How is Mrs. Caldwell?" Her grandparents' elderly neighbor had fallen last week, breaking her femur.

"She's doing well. She's still recovering from the surgery, but she was chatty last night when I brought her dinner. How was Levi this week?"

Jade smiled as she thought of him. "A mess. He fell into a horse trough yesterday."

"Good gracious. It's too cold for swimming."

Jade chuckled. "He learned his lesson. Even after drying off and getting a warm shower, he shivered until bedtime."

"What about his father?"

"Aaron is okay too." Jade wanted to say a lot more about Aaron, but her thoughts were still jumbled.

"Good."

As if sensing Jade's reluctance to talk more about Aaron, Gran politely said her good-byes and gave Jade space to process her wonderings.

She lowered her phone to her lap and cradled it there. She was lucky, really. Her grandparents lived on the other side of the world, and they had the ability to talk whenever they wanted. They could even video chat and send photos in an instant.

So, why did she miss them so much?

It wasn't a question she would ever be able to answer, but the reality bothered her. Shouldn't she be happy with what she had here?

Jade rolled the phone over in her hands and thought about Lauren's Sunday School lesson today. Was she following the Lord's plan for her life? Was she dreaming of Scotland when the Lord had sent her to Blackwater with a purpose?

As she turned the phone, the screen faced her again and lit up, revealing a text notification from Aaron. She opened the message and read.

Aaron: Are you okay? Do you need me?

Jade released a contented breath. It was the message he'd sent her after she snuck off to help Lauren with the kids. Aaron was a good man, a caring father, and a hard worker. She wasn't sure how she'd ended up on his doorstep, but the moving and shaking of her life until now seemed disjointed. Had she missed out on some great people and relationships in life because she hadn't stuck around long enough?

She tucked her chin and said a silent prayer.

Lord, I pray that You would guide me. Let my heart lead me in the path You have chosen for my life.

Dixie rested her head on Jade's knees, and she looked up just as the door behind her opened. She turned as the happy voices inside filled the once-quiet space where she sat on the front porch.

Aaron stepped out and closed the door behind him, but she was already getting to her feet.

"Hey, everything okay?"

Jade nodded. "Yeah. It was Gran, and we had a little to catch up on. I haven't talked to her all week." She smiled. He had texted her earlier when he couldn't find her at church, and now he was checking on her again. "Did you eat without me?"

Aaron wrapped his arm around her shoulder and kissed the top of her head. "I didn't, but I'm getting weak with hunger."

Her feelings for Aaron weren't all that confusing, they just weren't simple. She cared deeply about him and his son, but would building a life here mean forgetting her dream and her family?

Chapter Eleven

AARON

Aaron and Weston matched Hunter's pace as they homed in on the calf. It was time to separate the calves from their mothers, and they'd been roping the skittish calves all afternoon.

On foot, Hunter was able to dart quickly when a calf changed course on a dime. Aaron stayed a little farther back and dictated the overall direction they were headed. They'd done this hundreds of times, but it still felt more like an art than a science.

Hunter jogged at a steady pace through the thin snow. His hot breaths formed a continuous cloud in the cold air.

Weston was going to give out before Hunter did. The older horse wasn't built for this kind of work anymore. Aaron regretted his mount choice but slowed the pace to a walk. It would take longer to cool the old horse down when they were finished separating the herd.

Aaron signaled to Hunter to slow down, knowing full-well it would mean they'd be wrangling calves until suppertime.

Hours later, Aaron, Hunter, and Weston were drenched in cold sweat as they entered the stables.

Maddie met them at the north bay door. "I was wondering when you were bringing my baby back." She brushed a hand down Weston's wet mane.

"Sorry for runnin' him so hard today. I forgot he's an old-timer," Aaron said as he slung his leg over to dismount.

"That's okay. I'll walk him until he cools down." She patted Weston's cheek and crooned at the horse, "Then I'll pamper you the way you like. You can sleep inside tonight."

Hunter strode toward the nearby sink. "Do you have to talk to the horses like they're babies?"

"Yes. Because they're *my* babies," Maddie said.

Hunter shook his head and rubbed the grease cutter soap up to his elbows.

Aaron pulled his phone from his pocket and saw a text from Jade.

Jade: Do you have any old tires I could use? I'm at the main house.

Aaron lifted his head to Maddie. "Hey, can I cut out? Jade needs me to find some tires."

Maddie waved her hand in the air. "Bye. See you at supper."

Aaron texted Jade back asking for some time to locate them. He was pretty sure there were a few in the old shed on the eastern side of the ranch.

He jumped in his truck and threw his hat on the bench seat beside him. It would be dark by the time he made it back to the main house, and he'd be even later if he couldn't find the tires Jade needed.

Before he reached the shed, he got another text from Jade.

Jade: Any stakes? And some rope, please.

He wasn't sure what she was up to, but he'd bet his last paycheck it had something to do with Levi. With Jade and Levi together every day, he never knew what he was going to come home to.

He found four tires and a thick rope but no stakes. He grabbed a few metal fence posts in case her plan could be altered.

It was full dark before he pulled up at the main house. He left the supplies in the truck to look for Jade.

In the meeting room, he spotted her instantly playing Mother May I with Levi and four other kids. They laughed and shouted as one of the kids forgot to ask permission before moving.

When she spotted him, she waved him over.

"Hey, I got the tires and the rope, but no stakes."

She shrugged. "That's fine. Thanks for bringing it. I may need your help first thing in the morning too."

"What are you up to?" Aaron asked.

She held up a silencing finger. "Hold that thought. I need to wrap up this game."

He kissed her on the forehead and made his way to the washing station to clean up before supper.

Minutes later, Jade found him and wrapped her arms around his middle. "My hero."

Aaron chuckled. "Care to share? I'm worried I've made myself an accomplice to a crime."

"Not a crime. I want to set up an obstacle course for the kids. Kaylee and Sawyer aren't leaving until Thursday, and Hattie, Tiffany, and

Ava are here until Saturday. I told their parents they could hang out with Levi and me so they could do some trail rides with Lucas and Maddie while they're here."

"That's a great idea. You sure you don't mind adding a handful of kids to your days?"

"Not at all. We had a blast today, but now I have to line up some things we can do this week." She tapped Aaron's nose. "That's where you come in. I need your big muscles to do some heavy lifting."

He narrowed his eyes at her. "Is that why you keep me around?"

Jade lifted one shoulder. "It's one reason. It helps that you're handsome."

"That may be a problem. I plan to go gray soon, and my left knee is already giving me fits. I might need a replacement."

She stroked his cheek with a grin. "That's okay. I'll take care of you when your hair turns gray and you fall apart."

The image of Jade still being here when he was old struck a chord in his heart. "That's a long time to hang around."

"Not really," Jade said. "Cowboys age faster than regular men."

Aaron laughed and wrapped a hand around her shoulder. "Let's eat or I won't make it to thirty."

The visiting kids spotted Jade and huddled around her as they stood in line. She helped each of them fill their plates and sent them to find seats at the tables. Aaron watched as she mothered children she'd only met this morning. They had already attached themselves to her, labeling her their leader.

In the morning, he'd wake early to run by the stables and the pole barn on the western perimeter. If Jade wanted an obstacle course, she'd get only the best. He mentally logged the list of things he could build as soon as the sun came up.

Chapter Twelve

JADE

Jade circled a word. "What about this one?"

Levi studied it. "Plan."

"Correct."

"And this one." She circled another word in the list of dozens on the page.

"Truck."

"Great job."

Levi held up a hand. "How much longer until we get to do math?"

Jade tapped a finger against her jaw as if contemplating her response. "How about you count the letters in each word you read correctly until we finish this class?"

Levi sat up straighter. "Okay."

"This word."

Levi only hesitated a moment. "Lion."

"Correct."

She waited as he counted the letters. "Four letters."

"Why don't we keep track of the number of letters in each word and add them together at the end? Then you'll be able to see how many letters you read."

"Oh, yeah," Levi said, pencil in hand.

"Let's try a sentence." She printed a three-word sentence in front of Levi.

His eyes widened as he read, "I love you."

"Correct again. You're a quick learner. You'll be reading the bulletin board in the meeting room before long." The covered corkboard had fascinated Jade since her arrival. She hadn't known the extent of the ranching industry before coming to Blackwater, but she could see why Levi and his uncles liked it here. It was their home, but they put their hearts and souls into the land God had provided.

"One, four, three," Levi said, looking up at Jade. "That means I love you."

Jade gently bumped her shoulder against his. "Sometimes, I love you is more than words. Sometimes, people tell us they care about us in different ways. So, I think 143 can certainly mean I love you."

Levi nodded. "What's the next word?"

"This is a tough one." She circled a word on the page.

"Jump," Levi said.

"Good job."

"Is it math time yet?" he asked again.

"Bud, we already did your math lesson today. First thing this morning."

He rested his chin in his hand. "I know, but I like numbers better than letters."

"That's okay. I like vegetables more than fruits."

Levi laughed. "No, you don't."

"I do! Always have."

Aaron's steady footsteps thudded on the porch outside, and Levi jumped up.

"Daddy's back!"

Jade gathered up the class materials as Aaron walked in and wrapped Levi in a hug.

"Have you grown since lunch? I swear you were only this tall earlier, but now you're this tall." Aaron held up a hand, measuring the shorter and taller heights.

"I don't think I grew, but I read a bunch of words with Jade."

Aaron turned his attention to Jade, and her chest flooded with warmth. Would she ever get used to melting every time he looked her way?

The man had a captivating stare that drew her in from across the room.

Aaron patted Levi's shoulder. "Go get ready for bed."

"I can get ready for bed in just three minutes," Levi said.

"I don't know about that. You'll have to show me."

Levi stepped up to an invisible starting line and bent forward at the waist. "Time me, Dad."

Aaron pulled his phone from his back pocket and tapped the screen. "Ready, set, go."

Levi rushed off to his room and closed the door behind him.

Aaron hung his hat on the rack by the door and brushed a hand over his hair. "That kid's a mess."

Jade slid the papers she and Levi had written on into a folder and tucked it into her small messenger bag. "Agreed, but he's a sweet mess."

Aaron rolled his eyes, but the slight lift of his mouth gave away his amusement. "If you say so."

"I do. He was so good today, and we had so much fun."

Aaron wrapped his arms around her and pulled her close. "I'm glad."

He pressed a kiss to her forehead and lingered. The thick smell of burning wood and smoke filled her nose as she breathed deep.

"Have you been around a fire?"

"Yeah, we burned a dead tree in the north pasture."

Levi's bedroom door flew open. Aaron backed away from Jade in a flash, but Levi didn't pay them any attention as he darted into the bathroom and closed the door behind him.

Jade covered her mouth with her hands as she laughed. "You think this is funny?" he asked, but the question didn't hold any sting.

"I do. You're like a teenager afraid of getting caught by his parents," she said around her laughter.

"Well, that's kind of how I feel."

Jade patted her hand against his chest—the rock-solid surface she loved to nuzzle against on Aaron's couch after Levi went to bed. She liked to lay her head there and listen to Aaron tell her about the sweet and funny things Levi had done when he was younger.

She stretched up onto her toes and planted a sweet kiss on the corner of his mouth. "I get it. I don't think we should tell him yet either."

"You know it isn't anything against you, right? I just—"

She placed a finger over his lips. "I know. You have to be careful and sure, I agree with you."

When she slowly lowered her finger, Aaron stayed still.

"Wow. That was easy." He narrowed his eyes at her. "Are you sure you're real?"

Jade threw her head back and laughed.

Levi burst out of the bathroom dressed in blue pajamas with running horses all over them. "Done! Dad, stop the clock!"

Aaron found his phone and stopped the timer. "One minute and thirty seconds. That's half of three minutes."

"I did it!" Levi punched the air in celebration.

"Well, you said you would," Jade said. "I knew you could do it, Levi Benjamin Harding."

Levi laughed and turned to his dad. "She can't guess my middle name."

Jade put her hands on her hips. "I'll get it right one of these days."

Levi grabbed her hand. "Will you tuck me in?"

Jade tilted her head. "But I tucked you in last night. I think it's your dad's turn."

"Yeah," Aaron said. "I'm feeling a little forgotten and unloved."

"Okay, Dad can tuck me in tonight, but can you tuck me in tomorrow night?" Levi asked.

"Sure can. I'll see you in the morning." She wrapped her arms around Levi and squeezed tight.

Before either of them let go, Levi whispered into her hair, "One, four, three."

Hot tears stung the back of Jade's eyes, appearing so quickly that she couldn't prepare for the purge.

She hadn't been prepared for Levi's love, though hers had been waiting patiently in the wings for Levi's genuine acceptance.

"One, four, three," she whispered back past her constricting throat before releasing Levi and quickly wiping her tears on the sleeve of her shirt. "Good night. See you in the morning."

"Night, Jade," Levi said as he darted off toward his room.

Aaron pulled her in and kissed her hard, yet slow and sweet. She was breathless by the time he released her.

"Good night," he whispered low and deep.

"Good night."

He followed her out to the porch, and she knew he would watch her until she closed the door to her cabin.

She walked through her nightly routine in a stunned daze. Levi loved her, and she loved him back.

In the quiet of her bedroom, she turned off the light and climbed into bed. She reached for the rock Levi had given her on the bedside table and rubbed her fingertips over the smooth surface.

As she did every night, she whispered a prayer, "Dear God, I pray that You would guide my heart." She swallowed hard. "I'm scared. A little boy loves me, and I love him more than I understand. The problem is that I love his dad too, and I... I'm scared. I've never loved anyone like that before, and I haven't been cherished by a man the way Aaron cherishes me."

With her eyes closed, she shook her head and continued turning the rock in her hands. "I don't know where I belong. I've always gone where the wind took me, but I don't think I've ever asked You where I should be. I feel something here with these people. It's different, and I don't know what it is. That's why I'm calling on You, Lord. Please help me to see the path You have laid for me. All my life I've wanted to live and work in Scotland. I miss my gran, and I wish I could see her more often."

Jade exhaled in a rush. "But You've shown me this beautiful place with these wonderful people, and I'm ridiculously happy. I love them, Lord. Have I been chasing the wrong dream? Have I been running away from You?" She clutched the rock to her chest. "I don't know where I belong. Help me, please."

She tossed and turned until after midnight, wishing she could call her grandmother, her sister, her mother, or someone who could help her. But in her heart she knew that none of them could. She felt displaced and unsure, but she knew she would have to wait on the Lord to guide her home.

Chapter Thirteen

AARON

Aaron watched Levi scurry to the serving counter after lunch. Mama Harding's fingers had barely clasped the plate Levi handed her before he darted toward the exit.

Standing to intercept him, Aaron hurried to the door. "Hold up. You have to change clothes before you play outside."

Levi groaned. "I'll stay clean."

"Not a chance. Every other shirt you own is stained. I'm not risking your church clothes."

Levi threw his head back. "Okay. Can we go home so I can change?"

"Just a minute. Take a seat."

Levi trudged back to the seat he'd vacated beside Jade.

"Sitting on ready?" she asked.

"Yes," Levi said with a huff.

"I think your dad is almost finished eating. It won't be long," Jade assured him.

Aaron shouldn't be surprised that Levi responded better to Jade. Her patience hadn't wavered in the months she'd been at Blackwater. She was past proving her unwavering kindness, and Aaron was certain the Lord had sent her to the ranch when he and Levi had needed her most.

After lunch, Aaron, Jade, and Levi changed out of their Sunday best and into layers to ward off the frigid November weather.

Levi's jacket was barely zipped before he took off running for the truck.

Jade wrapped her heavy coat tighter around her middle. "He really loves that playground. It's been a long time since I've been this cold."

Aaron tsked. "I wish I could say this is the worst of it, but it'll probably get colder this year."

"You think we'll have a white Christmas?" Jade asked.

She looked up at him with those pale-blue eyes he loved, and he needed to pinch himself. The beautiful, kind Jade Smith was talking about spending Christmas with him and his son, and he didn't deserve this level of happiness.

"I think it's safe to say we will. Decembers here are brutal."

They piled into Aaron's truck and drove back to the main house. Levi ran to the playground that had grown to include monkey bars and a seesaw, plus the climbing dome and swing set he'd gotten for his birthday.

Aaron and Jade settled into their usual swing that faced the side yard. He'd bought it from Grady's a month ago when Jade confessed she wished they could sit closer together while they watched Levi. The old rocking chairs they'd sat in before were still nearby.

"Hey, Dad," Levi shouted.

Aaron turned his attention to Levi just in time to see him mouth what looked like "I love you."

"Love you too," Aaron replied.

Levi laughed. "I said olive juice!"

Jade snickered beside Aaron.

"Did you teach him that?" he asked as he wrapped his arm around her shoulders and pulled her in close to his side.

"Maybe. Probably." Her innocent response was amplified when she brushed her fair blonde hair over one shoulder.

After climbing, running, and sliding for a few minutes, Levi ran up to Jade and whispered something in her ear before rushing away without looking back.

She turned to Aaron and shrugged. "What?"

"Are you going to tell me what he said?"

Her gaze darted to Levi who was counting as he swung back and forth.

"One, four, three," Jade said.

"What does that mean?" Why had Levi run all the way over here to whisper the three numbers?

Jade's indecision wasn't helping his curiosity.

She finally said, "It means I love you."

He should have seen this coming, should have known Levi would love Jade.

He *had* known it was coming, but it hadn't prepared him for the surge of his own love for both Jade and his son. "Of course he loves you."

Her lips tugged in an uneasy smile. "I love him too."

Aaron pulled Jade in and wrapped both arms around her. He buried his face in her hair and held her. They'd only recently opened up to Levi about their budding relationship, and he seemed completely unfazed by the change as if he'd expected it.

It would be pathetic if he told Jade he loved her now. He'd been shown up by his own son. Plus, he wanted the first time he told her that she was the love of his life to be special, not on the playground. It screamed elementary crush.

Aaron kissed the top of her head before loosening his hold on her. "You know, I used to be able to count the people I could depend on in this world on two hands." He let his gaze brush over the simple arch of her brows, the straight angle of her nose, and the soft curve of her lips. "I recently ran out of fingers."

Jade clicked her tongue behind her teeth. "Might need to take your socks off. You have ten toes."

Aaron watched Levi playing. He loved his son so much his chest ached. "I thought I was bad at it."

Jade tilted her chin up. "At what?"

"Being in a relationship. Levi's mom, Christina, was the only real relationship I've had, and I did a lot of messing up."

Jade laid her head on his shoulder. "We all mess up."

Aaron huffed a laugh. Leave it to Jade to tell it like it is. "I didn't know how to read her. Didn't know how to talk to her. I was clueless about everything." He swallowed and let the anger and fear wash over him. "Then she left, and I knew it was my fault. It was because I didn't know my left foot from my right, and she was tired of waiting around for me to figure it out. The problem is, I still don't know what to do."

Jade stretched to kiss his cheek. "You don't have to do anything. Just be yourself. When you're being yourself, I see how much you care about Levi, I see you work hard for him, and I see you worry about me and how I'm settling in here. You care so much about others, and that's a big part of being in a relationship." She nuzzled the crook between his neck and shoulder.

He wanted her to be right. For the sake of their future together, he hoped she was. He didn't have much else to offer her.

Jade continued. "That's what you need to do. Be yourself. Because you're doing great when you don't overthink it. You listen, you care, and you put your family first. You're so good at this, and you didn't even know it."

She lifted her head to look at him, and adoration showed in her eyes. "She missed out. She walked out on a good thing, and that was her loss."

The talk of Christina should have affected him, but it didn't this time. The newfound contentment he'd found with Jade overpowered old hurts.

Jade slid her gloved hand into his and squeezed. "She wouldn't have been happy here.

She wanted something else, and nothing you did could have changed that."

Suddenly, the air left his lungs. They tightened within him, rebelling and refusing to do their part to keep him alive.

Christina may have wanted something else, but Jade did too. She wanted to be with her grandmother, and she wanted to teach children on the other side of the world.

And if she wanted that dream more than she wanted him or Levi, there was nothing he could do to keep her here.

He searched his memories. When was the last time Jade had mentioned Scotland? A month ago? A few weeks? He'd noticed that when she mentioned waiting for an available teaching position, she didn't talk about it as something she was still striving to achieve. Did that mean she was happy here? Was she happy *enough* here? What would it take to overshadow her lifelong dream?

Jade whispered, "She couldn't see your worth because she wasn't looking at you. That was her problem."

Was Jade telling him that she was looking for a future here? Was he only hearing what he wanted to hear? Was it wise to hope so much when he had no real control over her final decision?

Did he even want to believe her words? He was bound to be disappointed if he formed expectations.

He loved her, and it had happened without his consent. He didn't want to accept the terrifying possibility that he may have found the one woman he would love for the rest of his life only to lose her to an invisible dream.

Chapter Fourteen

JADE

Jade held her hands over her eyes as she counted aloud. She couldn't see the ten-foot-tall stack of square hay bales to her left, but the earthy smell filled her nose.

She heard Levi scurrying around the north barn in search of a hiding place. As she counted down, the rustling grew more frenzied.

"Three, two, one. Ready or not, here I come."

The sounds of movement had disappeared, leaving her without a clue where to begin looking. Levi was exceptionally good at hide-and-seek, and he was only getting better. He knew the best places to hide in every barn on the ranch.

She peeked around a tractor, but Levi wasn't there. She continued her search around and under every piece of equipment with still no sign of him.

"Levi?"

She'd checked everywhere. He had to be here somewhere. He knew not to leave the barn without her. She moved quicker through the barn the second time. Pushing down the rising panic, she double and triple checked every possible place.

"Levi, please come out. I can't find you. You win." She turned, scanning every inch of the pole barn.

"Boo!" Levi screamed as he jumped out from behind a tractor.

Jade jerked back, a hand flying to her chest to contain her racing heart.

Levi pointed and laughed. "I got you!"

Her chest rose and fell in large swells. "Please don't scare me like that."

Levi was still laughing as he stepped back. He didn't see the harrowing disc behind him, but his smile died in an instant when the metal bar that encased the dangerous equipment hit the back of his leg.

He'd told her the names and uses for every piece of equipment in this barn, and the harrowing disc had cemented a place in her mind. It was by far the most dangerous with its sharp, circular blades.

Adrenaline was already coursing through Jade's body from Levi's scare. When his expression turned to a look of blind fear, she lunged without thinking. Levi was falling backward, and her balance was lost when she extended to reach him. She grabbed his shoulders and threw him to the side, away from the line of blades.

She reached for the bar that surrounded the discs, but she was falling too fast. Her hand landed on the cold metal just as the nearest blade sliced through her arm just below her shoulder.

Pain shot through her arm, blinding and hot, at the same time the bar she held crashed into her ribs.

She cried out, but her lungs were stalled. Panic engulfed pain as the need to breathe intensified.

"Jade!" It was Levi, but he sounded so far away.

Someone screamed her name again, but she couldn't respond. There wasn't any air to speak.

Slowly, she turned her head toward the pain in her arm. The blade was stuck at least an inch into her skin, but there wasn't much blood. The hopeful part of her brain said this might not be so bad. It didn't look bad if she ignored the throbbing in her arm.

But her realistic side said this was worse than it seemed. Everything was spinning, and sparks flashed in her vision.

"Jade! Daddy's coming!"

"Wh—?" She didn't have the strength to utter a whole word.

"Jade! I'm sorry!" His words were muffled as if she were hearing them under water.

She inched back, but the pain surged with the movement. The fire in her arm was white hot as blood began gushing from the opening in her skin.

Stars danced in her vision, and she heard Levi crying.

Levi needed her. She had to go to him. Where was he? She couldn't let anything happen to him.

Her vision blurred, darkening from the edges inward to a quickly vanishing spot of light.

"Help." It took every ounce of energy and concentration to speak the word. Help for herself or help for Levi? She wasn't sure. Was he injured? He was crying.

The small circle of light disappeared, and everything slipped into darkness.

***

Roaring filled her ears, and flashes of white pulsed behind her closed eyelids. She squeezed her eyes closed, unwilling to let the harsh light in.

It hurt. It hurt to breathe, hurt to furrow her brow against the onslaught.

"Jade?"

That was Aaron's voice. She could open her eyes for him. She needed to see him more than she needed a reprieve from the pain.

She squinted, closing her eyes at intervals to rest, before opening them and allowing the light in.

"Aaron."

He was at her side, leaning over her and blocking the light that blinded her.

"I'm here. Do you need more pain relievers?"

She looked to one side and then the other without moving her head. "I don't know."

His fingertips brushed down the side of her face, rough and calloused against her smooth cheek. "They closed the wound. You'll be on powerful antibiotics for a while, but the doctor said you shouldn't lose any range of motion or capabilities." His gaze darted to her arm. "You'll have to be careful and rest for a while."

She couldn't look. The memory of falling without hope of dodging the oncoming blade was too fresh in her mind. The helplessness and fear threatened to crawl back up her throat. She'd effectively pushed them down into the pit of her stomach for a moment, but they were alive and well now.

"I'm tired," she whispered.

His hand rested on her uninjured shoulder. "Rest. I'll be right here."

"Levi?" she asked, tired and waning.

"He's fine. He's with Maddie." Aaron's jaw tightened. "You scared him."

"He scared me," she said.

Aaron's gaze fell to her shoulder where his hand rested. "He told me what you did."

Confusion clouded her thoughts. "What did I do?" Had she left him? Was he hurt? Had she failed to push him far enough away from the discs?

"You saved him." Aaron swallowed hard. "I can't think about what could have happened to him if you hadn't saved him."

Aaron loved his son with his whole heart, but she'd never seen him so wrought with emotion.

"Is he okay?" she asked.

"He's great, thanks to you."

Those words seeped into her skin and settled in her heart, calming her worst fears.

"Good." Her eyes drifted closed, and they were too heavy to open again.

Aaron's warm lips brushed her cheek, and he whispered something that she couldn't make out before she fell back into sleep.

Chapter Fifteen

AARON

Aaron snuck another glance at Jade as he drove toward Blackwater Ranch. He was thankful she'd been discharged from the hospital. They were both tired and ready to be home.

She was still uncomfortable, though she promised him the pain wasn't nearly as bad anymore. Still, the thought of her enduring even a small dose of pain had his stomach turning.

"Are you okay?" he asked for the third time.

She rested her head back against the seat. "I'm fine. Just ready to be home. I miss Levi and everyone else."

He laid his hand over hers. "I know. But remember, the doctor said take it easy."

"Aaron, you can stop now. I'll be fine. I'm not lifting weights or anything like that."

He swallowed and cleared his throat. Why did it feel like he was being choked? "I know. I just hate this."

"That makes two of us. I'm just grateful it wasn't Levi."

Aaron picked up her hand and pressed his lips to the back. "Thank you. I can't tell you how much it means to me that you saved him, but I still hate what happened to you."

"Stop it," Jade said. "Levi would have been much worse off."

He turned his truck toward the cabins, but she stopped him. "Wait, I want to see Levi."

"Are you sure? You need to rest."

"I'm sure. I miss him."

Aaron turned the steering wheel and headed for the main house. It was bound to be loud and crowded at this time of day. Lunch was just starting, and everyone would be eager to see Jade. They'd given her space while she was in the hospital, but the Hardings, especially the women, weren't patient.

Aaron helped her out of the truck. She was slow moving with two broken ribs and one arm in a sling, but Aaron would be the most attentive assistant. Even if she hadn't sacrificed her health to save his son, he would care for her every day in the best way he knew how—with his devotion.

Inside the main house, Aaron gently pulled her coat from where it hung over her shoulders. They had barely made it inside before Levi spotted them.

"Jade!"

She turned at Levi's call, and the energetic light she'd been missing the last few days returned. "Levi Theodore Harding!"

Aaron barely caught Levi by the collar before he crashed into Jade. "Hold up. We have some rules."

Levi looked up at his dad. "I said I was sorry. No more hiding."

"Not that. Jade's arm and side hurt really bad, so you need to be careful about touching or bumping into her."

Jade slowly squatted to Levi's level. The movement caused the familiar sharp pain in her side. "Gentle hugs are still very welcome."

Levi tentatively wrapped his arms around her neck. "I'm glad you're home."

"Me too. I missed you."

Levi leaned back but kept his arms around her neck. "I missed you too."

Jade wiped her hand over his cheek. "I'm fine. It was all an accident. No one is to blame." She pulled him in again with her left arm. "I'm so glad you're okay."

Levi held on longer this time. Others stood nearby, waiting to welcome Jade home. She said a few greetings before Aaron ushered her through the crowd, leading her with a gentle hand on the small of her back.

"Jade needs to eat. Then she needs rest."

Everyone backed away while Aaron heaped double helpings of everything onto a plate for her. She assured everyone that she was feeling much better, but Aaron could see the exhaustion in her eyes. It had been a long and painful few days for her. Tests, medications, and monitoring one right after the other.

After dinner, Aaron stood, grabbing his plate and Jade's. He looked to Levi. "Tell Jade good night."

"Right now? It's too early for bed," Levi whined.

"It is for you, but not for her. She's tired."

Levi inspected her and seemed to accept his dad's words. "Okay. Good night." Levi barely wrapped his arm over her shoulder and whispered, "One, four, three."

"Good night. See you in the morning." She cupped her hand over his cheek. "One, four, three."

"Are we having school tomorrow?" he asked hopefully.

Aaron laid a hand on his son's shoulder. "Not tomorrow, bud. She needs to get well."

"Okay," Levi said, though it was clear he was disappointed.

"I'll still be around, but I might not be able to get your lessons together just yet. It should only be a few days."

Aaron narrowed his eyes at her. "We'll see. Your time off is paid, and I think you need more than a few days to heal from this."

Jade shrugged. "We could do some simple things. And we don't have to play rough or anything. We could play some board games or something."

"We'll see how you're feeling. Don't commit yourself to anything," Aaron said.

They quickly said their farewells to everyone else. He could tell Jade's energy was fading fast. She hadn't been up and moving around much since the accident, and almost every move evoked a grimace of pain.

Aaron helped her inside her cabin and onto the couch where she wanted to sit. He brought her overnight bag and purse in while she rested her head against the back of the couch.

After putting her things in her bedroom, he checked the log rack. He leaned over and kissed her forehead. "I'm going to grab some firewood. I'll be right back."

She only nodded, and he jogged to his truck before peeling off toward the firewood shed. He loaded the logs in record time, eager to get back to Jade's side.

When he returned carrying the first armload of wood, she was quiet and still on the couch. After unloading the firewood, he leaned over Jade to check on her before heading out for another armload. She looked peaceful in sleep.

Just as he pressed his lips to her cheek, her eyes opened. "Are you leaving?"

"I was going to grab some more wood and then build you a fire, but I can stay longer if you want."

"Please. I just... I don't know."

Aaron sat on the couch beside her. "Would you feel more comfortable staying with me for a while? You can have my bed, and I'll take the couch."

"Oh, no. I couldn't."

He held up a hand. "I promise I wasn't offering just because I want you to stay with me. I want to be close in case you need anything. You can't even sit up from lying on your own right now. What would you do if you needed to get out of bed in the night?"

Jade's lips shifted to one side, then the other. "I hadn't thought of that."

"They mentioned it during your discharge orders," he said.

"I guess I just thought it would be easier than this."

Aaron picked up her hand and rubbed circles on the back. "You can stay with Noah and Camille if you'd be more comfortable with that."

Jade laughed. "They didn't invite me."

"They would take you in without hesitating. Have you met them?"

She smiled. "You're right. But I think I'd like to stay with you. We already have a routine together. Plus, I could walk a few steps back to my cabin if I needed anything."

"You mean I could go get anything you need. Your job right now is resting and telling me what you want me to do."

"I'm not helpless."

"I still want to take care of you."

She tilted her head and gave him a look of pity. "How are you handling this?"

By *this*, she meant the crushing fact that had Levi fallen on the blade, the injury would likely have been fatal.

"I just—" He couldn't even finish the thought.

She leaned over a few inches to kiss his cheek, but he wanted more than a quick brush of her lips against his skin. He angled his head to catch her mouth with his and kissed her sweet and gentle.

He cradled her head and leaned forward so she could rest her back against the couch. He drank her in, savoring the feel of her lips against his and her skin beneath his fingertips.

He could have lost her, could be alone and heartbroken with a son who didn't understand loss. The alternative to adoring her like this would have broken him.

When the kiss ended, he rested his forehead against hers and whispered, "One, four, three."

She lifted her head, and her eyes opened wide. "What?"

Aaron brushed his thumb over the angle of her jaw. "I love you. One, four, three. In words or numbers, I love you."

Jade tucked her lips between her teeth, and her hazy blue eyes turned glassy.

"I love the way you love Levi. I love your kindness, and the way you seem to always understand everyone. Because you're always thinking of others first. I love all of you and everything about you." His voice shook as he continued. "I'm terrified to love you, but I can't stop."

Jade rested her fingertips on his lips. "I love you too."

Happiness filled him until his chest grew tight. He'd hoped she felt the same about him, but now he knew for sure. Jade didn't skirt the truth or tell falsehoods to spare feelings.

Aaron brushed a single tear from beneath her lashes. Her beauty often struck him speechless, and it was easy to get lost in her eyes when she looked at him as if he meant the world to her.

He kissed her again and the world tilted around them. Jade loved him, and he didn't need anything else. She was the one for him, she was the one for Levi, and she was the one who would stay because she loved them too.

Chapter Sixteen

JADE

The following week was tougher than Jade had expected. Pain and exhaustion followed her everywhere.

That was how she'd ended up spending most afternoons napping in the living room at the main house. Her energy held until after lunch when the pain medication wore off and her muscles were exhausted from tensing in pain for hours.

She'd been a complete lazy bones through Thanksgiving, but she hadn't had enough strength to properly shower, much less help roast a turkey. Thankfully, the Hardings had prepared a feast for the family, ranch workers, and guests. She'd slept more than usual that weekend, and the whole holiday was a blur. Aaron had tended to her hand

and foot, and Levi was extra helpful too, dutifully mimicking his dad.

Jade didn't feel the usual after-lunch lethargy today and grabbed a rag to wipe down the cleared tables.

Maddie appeared at Jade's side, and she jumped, clutching her chest just as she had when Levi had scared her in the barn.

"Goodness. You startled me."

Maddie placed a comforting hand on Jade's uninjured arm. "Sorry about that. I thought you heard me walk up."

"No problem. I was just lost in my own thoughts. What's up?"

Maddie's hand raked over the blonde braid that hung over her shoulder. She was exceptionally beautiful, but the horse trainer was more interested in tending the stables than getting gussied up. Still, her friendliness only made her more likable.

"Are you feeling better? You've been up and about a little more than usual today."

"I'm feeling pretty good today," Jade answered with a smile.

Maddie slipped one hand into the back pocket of her jeans and pointed with her other. "Good. I was wondering if you wanted to get out of the house and come to the stables with me.

Nothing strenuous. I was just thinking you'd like a change of scenery."

"I'd love that." Jade usually spent the time between her nap and supper planning Levi's lessons, but she was thoroughly caught up. They divided their school hours between the mornings and evenings, since Aaron insisted she rest in the middle of the day.

"Great. Let me get some things together, and I'll come pick you up in an hour."

"Thanks. I'm looking forward to it." Even if she wasn't feeling tired now, she'd need to use the next hour to rest if she intended to make it through an afternoon with Maddie and the horses.

Jade finished cleaning up the meeting room before excusing herself into the quiet living room. The pain in her side had been unbearable with every minute movement the first couple of weeks after her injury. Now, she could almost lower herself into the recliner without wincing.

While she couldn't sleep, she remembered she'd saved a link to a new homeschool curriculum she wanted to look into. She leaned over to lift her laptop from the nearby end table and squeezed her eyes closed against the pain. When would everyday activities get easier?

With her laptop open, she clicked straight to the link and fell into a rabbit hole of curriculums. She and Levi would never run out of things to do.

Jade checked the time and saw that she still had half an hour before Maddie would be back. She had plenty of time to clean out her email inbox. Cleaning out her inbox was just as satisfying as reaching a goal or marking a task off her to-do list. Anything important had a folder where it was saved. Anything spammy or smarmy got filed away in the trash.

A familiar notification email caught her eye. She'd opted to receive alerts for new openings on the Scottish job posting site, and she hurriedly clicked the listing. There hadn't been a new posting in months.

It was a primary teacher position, and she clicked rapidly to view the location. It was even close to Fort Augustus where her family lived.

With her heart pounding in her chest, she quickly completed the application. She'd grown familiar with the forms since graduating from the University of Glasgow with her teaching credentials.

She was finishing up the last page of the application when her phone rang. A photo of her grandmother standing in the doorway of the family restaurant filled the screen.

"Hey, Gran, guess what I'm doing?"

Her grandmother hummed in thought. "Teaching Levi how to make haggis?"

Jade laughed. "I'm not sure he'd be a fan of haggis, so I haven't tried that yet. Actually, I just finished up an application for a primary teacher position in the Highland school district. This one isn't too far from you."

"Oh, that's lovely. I didn't know you were still applying."

Jade bit her bottom lip and closed the application window on her laptop. "I haven't in a while, but there weren't any openings."

"I must have been mistaken. I thought you were happy in Blackwater."

"I am." Jade turned to the door where Maddie would appear soon. "I just got a little excited I guess."

"Then I'm excited for you also. I called to let you know that Mrs. Caldwell enjoyed the book you sent her."

Jade shut down her laptop and closed it. "That's great. I thought she'd be restless during her recovery time."

"She is. I can't imagine being bound to a chair for weeks," her grandmother said.

"Me either. I'm not as limited as Mrs. Caldwell, but I can say that not having good use of my arm and wincing in pain every time I turn is aggravating."

"I hope you're resting," Gran said in her sweet, nurturing tone.

"I am," Jade promised as she moved the laptop to the end table and gritted her teeth to stand from the recliner. "I didn't feel as tired today after lunch, so I'm supposed to be leaving any minute to see the horses with Maddie."

"I can't wait to hear about it."

Jade walked through the kitchen and into the meeting room, deciding to wait for Maddie there instead. She needed a few moments to stretch and stand before heading to the stables.

Christmas was only weeks away, and the large common room where the family, workers, and guests congregated was covered in garland, bows, and lights. A tall, decorated tree drew attention to the far corner of the room near the fireplace.

"This might be the first Christmas I haven't spent with you," Jade said.

"I know, but I'm sure you'll have a wonderful time with the Hardings."

Jade nodded, though her grandmother couldn't see her, the movement of acceptance helped her come to terms with spending Christmas without her family. "I know. We'll have a great time."

Maddie walked in, and Jade waved.

"I have to go, but I'll call you again soon."

"Bye. I love you."

"Love you too."

Maddie strode in with a smile shining beneath the wide brim of her hat. "Hey, you ready?"

"Ready." Jade carefully slipped her arms into her thick coat and followed Maddie to her truck. Stepping into the tall vehicle was a chore that left her panting.

"I'm sorry. I should have brought a different truck."

Jade waved a hand. "Oh, it's fine. I need to get used to doing normal things again."

"We'll take it slow today. Just let me know when you're ready for me to take you home."

They parked in front of the stables, and Jade clumsily slid out of the passenger seat feeling as if she'd accomplished some big task.

Inside, the large building smelled of leather and hay, and the air was markedly warmer than the frigid winter air outside.

Stalls filled the right side, and the left side of the building was lined with doors—some open and some closed. A few horses shuffled, curious about their presence.

Lucas stepped out of a nearby room carrying what looked to be a blanket covered in a red-and-green geometric pattern. "Hey, good to see you here," he said, stepping up to Jade's side and playfully bumping her uninjured arm with his shoulder. "Come to have some fun?"

"As much as I can tolerate. I'd love to ride one day, but I don't think that'll be an option for a while." Her hand instinctively moved to cover her aching ribs. The thought of jostling in a saddle made her stomach roll.

"That's okay," Maddie said as she stepped up to the closest stall and rubbed her hand up and down the neck of a brown horse. "I have just as much fun talking to the horses as I do riding." She nuzzled her cheek against the horse's. "Dolly is my best friend."

Lucas draped the blanket over the stall door and crossed his arms over his chest. "I thought I was your best friend."

Maddie leaned away from Dolly to kiss Lucas on the cheek. "Sorry, Dolly had me first."

Lucas feigned hurt as the corners of his mouth turned down. "I thought we had something special."

"We better! I didn't agree to love you for life just because you're charming."

Lucas tilted his head and turned to Jade. "She loves me."

Maddie's eyes grew wide. "Oh, I've been meaning to ask you what you think I should get Levi for Christmas."

Jade huffed. "That's a good question. I've been pondering it myself."

Lucas rolled his eyes. "I already told you, a slingshot."

Maddie furrowed her brow. "I'm not getting him a slingshot so he can pelt the horses with rocks. Your suggestion has been heard and declined."

Jade chuckled. "Agreed. Levi would be dangerous with a slingshot. Why don't you ask Aaron?"

Maddie reached into the pocket of her jacket and pulled out a horse treat. "Aaron has enough trouble coming up with something to get Levi. He probably doesn't have any extra ideas."

Jade leaned against the wall near Dolly's stall. "Sounds like another one of those things that's a lot harder as a single parent."

Maddie sighed. "It hasn't been easy for him, but we all try to help out. We're very thankful that you're here. Aaron seems a lot happier."

"It wouldn't have been any easier if Christina had stayed," Lucas said. "She wasn't very motherly."

With her hands on her hips, Maddie replied, "I can't imagine anyone who is a first-time mother is overly motherly in the beginning."

"No, not that. I don't know what it was, but she just didn't like it here. She always seemed trapped and tired."

Jade hadn't asked Aaron much about Christina, and as eager as she was to hear more, she didn't want to invade his privacy.

"The point is, she left Aaron and Levi one night without an explanation. They were better off without her. She was a runner, and nobody tried to stop her."

Jade brushed a hand down Dolly's mane. Did Aaron think she was a runner? *Was* she a runner? Could she leave them now after she'd fallen in love with both of them?

She thought about the application she'd submitted earlier and regretted it. She could have let the opportunity pass and never been the wiser, but when she saw the notification, it was her instinct to apply.

Lucas walked off, seemingly more upset than Jade had ever seen him.

Maddie's mouth quirked to one side. "He really hates that Christina left Aaron and Levi."

"I understand. No one deserves to be left like that," Jade said.

"Thankfully, they both have a lot of people who love them and they know they can count on. We stick together around here."

Jade nodded, feeling even worse for applying for the international job. She wasn't sure she even wanted it anymore. She'd just wanted it for so long that it became a habit. How could she leave them when she loved them so much?

She loved her family too, but her heart was here in Blackwater now.

Maddie pointed toward the feed room. "Let's grab some snacks and say our hellos to everyone."

Jade followed Maddie, feeling a surprising weight lifted from her shoulders. Any desire to leave this place and the people here was gone, and any word she heard from the job opening didn't matter anymore.

***

Levi studied the Skittles on the table in front of him. Jade had set out six colorful lines, and Levi was to continue the pattern with the candies. Her dad and Gran called them sweeties. She watched as he slid them around, and she checked his work as he went.

Soon, his head popped up. "Done!"

Jade pressed the button to stop the timer on her phone. "Great job. You beat your old time."

Levi insisted Jade time him on everything they did. He thrived on the pressure of beating a clock, and instead of crippling under pressure, his mind worked faster.

He punched the air with an exaggerated, "Yes!" before jumping from his seat to do a victory dance.

Aaron walked in the door just as Jade joined in.

"I missed my invitation to the party," he said, looking at Jade with that smile that sent her stomach flipping.

"I like to dance when I solve a problem," Levi said, turning in a circle and waving his hands in the air.

Aaron wrangled Levi as he continued to wiggle. "Why don't you get ready for bed?"

Levi nodded and continued his dance toward his bedroom. "Winner, winner, chicken dinner."

Jade laughed as he disappeared into his room. "I'm not sure what he thinks he won."

Aaron wrapped his arms around her and his mouth found hers as if they were magnetically charged.

Jade sighed as Aaron's kiss swept gently across her lips. Her hand rested on his jaw, feeling the movement as he kissed her. When his arm slid around the small of her back and pulled her closer, she lost her breath.

Her time spent with Levi was full of joy, but every moment in Aaron's arms was intimate and consumed with love. He adored her with longing looks, words of encouragement, and heartfelt appreciation. It was no wonder she found herself swept up in a rush of emotion every time he was near.

When he ended the kiss, she inhaled deep breaths. He was holding her still, but she felt as if she'd been running. A kiss had never been so exhilarating.

"Well, hello to you too," she said with a grin.

"How was your day?"

"Wonderful. Yours?" she asked.

"Better now."

Levi flung the bathroom door wide. "Dad, it's your turn to tuck me in!"

Aaron gently kissed her forehead. "I'll be right back."

Jade cleaned up their Skittle mess in the kitchen, and she'd just finished washing the coffee mugs in the sink when Aaron slid his arms around her waist.

Pressing his chest to her back, he whispered low in her ear, "I love you."

Warmth flooded her chest, but something else gnawed there. Guilt?

She turned in his arms and cradled his face in her hands. "We need to talk about a few things."

Aaron's eyes widened. "Uh-oh. That doesn't sound good."

"Well, it's not *bad*. I'm feeling a lot better now, and I don't really need help getting around anymore. I think it's time I moved back into the other cabin."

Aaron took a step back and moved his hands from her waist to hold her hands. "I'm sorry. I didn't mean to make you feel uncomfortable."

She shook her head. "You didn't. I never felt like you were pressuring me, but we're getting a little cozy here, and it feels very much like—"

"A family?" Aaron asked.

"Yes. A family." Uttering the word sent a shock of happiness from her fingertips to her toes. "And while I love you and Levi dearly, I'm not your wife." How badly she wanted to add "yet" to the end of that sentence.

Aaron wrapped his arms around her shoulders and tucked his face into the crook of her neck. "I understand. I should have thought of it myself. You moved in here because of your injury, and you're almost completely recovered now."

"Maybe tomorrow," she said with a chuckle. "I'm kind of tired tonight."

He kissed the top of her head. "I'll take care of it tomorrow."

She took a deep breath before moving on to the next order of business. She didn't want to tell him about the application she'd filled out this morning. He would be hurt if he knew she was still holding on to that old hope. And truly, she regretted the impulsive decision.

"I talked to my gran this morning. This is the first Christmas I haven't spent with her."

Aaron rubbed his hands up and down her arms. "Do you want to go?"

"Not for Christmas. I'd like to spend it here with you and Levi this year. But I would like to plan to visit her before spring. I know that's when things will get busier around here, and the same goes for my grandparents' restaurant. I want to spend some time with them before the tourist season picks up."

"Of course. Just let me know when you're going, and we'll manage here." He rubbed his jaw in thought. "You know you aren't stuck here, right? You can take time off whenever you need to get away."

"I'm not trying to get away," she assured him. "I truly like it here. I'm definitely not bored."

Aaron nodded, but his smile hadn't returned. Worry still marred his face. "Thinking about you leaving is scary."

She shook her head. "It's just for a few days—less than two weeks."

"I know, but we'll still miss you. And I'm not sure how we made it before without you. Moving you back into the other cabin is going to be difficult too."

Jade stretched up onto her toes and pressed her lips to his. His strong arms held her, unwilling to let her go.

Chapter Seventeen

AARON

The following morning, reality hit Aaron like a freight train. After Jade had mentioned visiting her family in Scotland, he'd spent most of the night staring at the ceiling. The couch wasn't built as a bed for a man over six-feet-tall, but he didn't mind it if it meant Jade was comfortable. It wasn't the sleeping environment keeping him awake. It was an old fear that had nothing to do with Jade and everything to do with his insecurities.

Years ago, Christina left without warning. Had there been signs he'd missed? He tried to remember that time before she left, but it was all a blur. He'd been thrown into the life of a single parent, and he'd been too busy trying to keep his head above water to worry about what he could have done better.

Now, Jade was here, and he didn't want her to leave. He trusted her when she said it was only for a few days. So why was he still worried? It was irrational. Jade was happy here. She loved him and Levi. Aaron put her, Levi, and his family second only to God in his life. He was all in.

Turning over pieces of sentences and worries in his mind lasted most of the night, leaving him dragging his feet even after breakfast and an extra cup of coffee.

Then the bull tore up the fence on the north pasture, and any hope of catching a break drove away laughing. There were wandering cows and rambunctious calves scattered for half a mile. Every hand on the ranch spent the day wrangling cattle.

The urgency of herding the cows back home and repairing the fence meant no one stopped for lunch or supper. He'd been able to call Jade in the afternoon to let her know he would be late getting in. She'd gladly agreed to put Levi to bed.

It was after nine in the evening when Aaron trudged to his cabin. Hungry and exhausted, he toed off his boots and dusted the mud from his jeans. He'd slid in the melting snow more than once today, covering his lower half in the slushy mess.

He slowly opened the door and was met with silence. The small table lamp by the couch was on and a fire burned in the fireplace, casting a dim glow over the living room.

As the door clicked closed behind him, Jade sat up from where she'd been lying on the couch. "Hey."

She rubbed her eyes the same way Levi did when he fought sleep. The innocence of the gesture had his chest aching. How blessed was he to be able to go about his day knowing that, no matter how rough things got on the ranch, his family was safe and warm?

His family. He'd been surrounded by family his whole life, but having Jade and Levi in this old cabin felt different.

She ran her fingers through her blonde hair, and he couldn't take his eyes off her. He wanted to tie his life to hers forever. He wanted her to be his wife, his friend, and his teammate for the rest of their lives. He'd worried all day about whether or not she might leave, but now that contemplation felt ridiculous.

He'd never been surer of anything in his life. When she left for Scotland, he'd have a talk with Levi, and they would go pick out a ring for her together. When she got back, he'd ask her to be his wife and Levi's mother.

He stepped over to the couch and whispered, "I didn't mean to wake you."

"It's fine. I wasn't sleeping soundly anyway. I wanted to wait up for you."

He sat on the couch beside her. His head fell back, and his eyes closed. He reached for her hand and kissed it gently. "Sorry I wasn't around today."

She scooted closer, resting her legs across his lap and snuggling close. He wrapped his arm around her shoulders and leaned his cheek on her head.

"It's okay," she whispered.

"I missed you." He spoke the words into her hair, breathing in the sweet scent that she'd brought into his home.

He lifted his head. "I'm sorry. I just remembered I was supposed to move your stuff back to your cabin today."

She laid a reassuring hand on his chest. "It's fine. I could have done it myself, but Levi and I stayed later than usual at the main house making Rice Krispie treats after supper."

Aaron hummed. "That sounds good."

She raised her head. "Oh, I brought you a plate of food from supper. I'll go heat it up."

He tightened his arms around her. "Please stay." He needed her more than he needed food right now.

"We brought you some Rice Krispie treats too."

"Thanks. I'll eat them for breakfast."

Neither of them moved, and Aaron had almost dozed off when Jade whispered, "What's your middle name?"

"Bennett. Why?"

"Just wondering. That's my grandfather's name."

"Really?" Aaron wanted to lift his head and talk more, but exhaustion was heavy in every limb of his body. "It was my great-great-grandfather's name. He founded the ranch."

"Is that why you chose it for Levi's middle name too?" she asked.

"Yes." He answered without thinking first. "Wait, have you known his name this whole time?"

"Of course. I keep his school records."

He hugged her tighter. "You're amazing."

She started to move away.

Aaron raised his head. "What are you doing?"

"You're tired. I thought you'd be ready for bed." She gestured to the couch. "You know, this is still your bed for one more night."

Aaron shook his head. "Not yet. Can you tell me more about your day?"

She rested her head on his shoulder. "I ordered Levi's Christmas present today."

His body and mind begged for sleep, but he fought against it. He wanted her to keep talking. Her voice was the most beautiful sound he'd ever heard. "What did you get him?"

"Walkie Talkies."

A single chuckle hummed in his chest. "He'll love that." His breathing grew shallow as he whispered, "Thank you for loving us."

He fought the exhaustion with his arms around Jade. He wasn't ready to let her go.

Chapter Eighteen

JADE

Jade removed the lid from the slow cooker and stirred the contents. Mama Harding's creamy potato soup was second to none, and the delicious smells of Christmas dinner filled the large kitchen at the main house. They'd been cooking since lunch, and there were still a few things left in the oven.

Haley walked past and inhaled a deep breath. "That smells amazing." Her stomach growled in agreement.

Laughing, Jade asked, "Do you need a bite before we leave?" If Haley was already hungry, she'd be uncomfortable through the candlelight service.

Haley opened a box of crackers and grabbed a handful. "This will tide me over."

Aaron stepped into the kitchen with Levi close behind him. They'd worn their Sunday best for the Christmas Eve candlelight service at church tonight.

Aaron slid his arm around Jade's waist and kissed her forehead. "You ready?"

She looked over her shoulder at Mama Harding. Camille, Laney, and Jade had helped with the cooking on and off all day, but Mama Harding hadn't stopped for more than five minutes since her feet hit the floor this morning.

"I think I'll ride over with your mom in a little bit. We still have a few things left to get ready."

Levi tugged on Aaron's belt. "Come on, Dad. Let's go." It was Levi's first Christmas Eve service at church, and he'd been jumping with excitement all week.

Aaron nodded. "I'll be out there in a minute."

Levi ran out of the kitchen without a backwards glance.

Aaron lifted Jade's hand to his lips and kissed her fingers. "I'll save you a seat. Thanks for helping out with dinner."

"Of course. I've had the best time today, and I've learned a thing or two about cooking."

Aaron's brows raised. "I'm impressed. You're already a great cook."

Jade brushed a hand over the collar of his shirt. "Thank you for saying so, but I'm average at best."

Aaron pressed a quick kiss to her lips before whispering, "Nothing about you is average, Jade."

The temperature in the kitchen rose five degrees, and she fought the urge to fan her face. Would she ever get used to Aaron's sweet adoration? Probably not, he never missed an opportunity to remind her of his devotion. "We'll be there soon. Love you."

"Love you too."

Jade turned to Mama Harding once everyone else had gone. "What's next?"

Mama Harding pointed as she wrapped the orange cake in aluminum foil. "The tablecloth and place mats are in that cabinet. The ones with the holly leaves on them."

Jade grabbed the table decorations and stepped out into the meeting room to set the tables. She'd never seen the ranch gathering place so empty before, but everyone was attending the church service tonight. Even the guests had gone.

Even without the lively sounds of a crowd, the room glowed with warmth. The fireplace burned low, and garland and ribbons hung throughout the room. Soon, this place would be bursting with celebration and cheer.

She covered the tables and returned to the kitchen. Mama Harding folded her apron and laid it on the counter before fluffing her gray-streaked hair.

"What can I do now?" Jade asked.

"Nothing. I think we're ready to go." Mama Harding brushed her hands down the front of her red-and-silver sweater. "I'll leave right before the end of the service and have a bit of time to get this set out before everyone gets here."

"I'll come with you," Jade said.

"Thank you, dear. You've been such a help today."

Jade turned off the lights as they stepped out of the kitchen. "I enjoyed it. I've been telling my grandparents about your cooking."

"How are they doing?" Mama Harding asked.

"Great. My parents have been there for a few days, and my sister and her family are flying out next week. Her husband couldn't get time off work until after Christmas this year."

They slid on their coats and scarves at the door. The sharp December wind whipped around them as they stepped outside.

"Want to take my van?" Jade asked.

"That would be wonderful. I don't like to drive at night," Mama Harding said.

Once they were closed inside the vehicle, Jade started the engine, and the windshield wipers pushed the fresh snow from the window.

Mama Harding broke the silence once they were on the main road. "I know you miss your family, but I'm glad to have you here with us."

Jade smiled, though it couldn't be seen in the darkness. "Thank you. I'm glad I'm here too. I do miss them, but I would miss this too."

"I haven't seen Aaron this happy in so long," Mama Harding whispered.

Jade sighed. "It hurts to think of what he went through. I haven't urged him to talk about Christina, but I don't know how she could have left them."

"Her sister died soon after she married Aaron."

Jade gasped. "I had no idea."

"She and her sister were very close, and the loss was too much for her. She grieved quietly by herself for a while, and Aaron gave her some space. He didn't know how to help her. None of us did. She was so closed off, we didn't know how to reach her. When they told us they were going to have a baby, we thought she was getting better. But when she had Levi, her sadness worsened. I tried to convince her to see a doctor, and she said she didn't want help. Sometimes, our best isn't enough. We found out a year later she'd died of a drug overdose. I guess she thought she needed a different kind of help than what we could give her."

"I'm so sorry." Jade hadn't realized Aaron's marriage had been shadowed in darkness from the beginning. He must have felt helpless. "Lucas said no one tried to stop her when she left."

"That's not true. She'd withdrawn from the family so much before she left that Lucas may have assumed we'd given up on her, but we tried. Silas, Aaron, and I did everything we could to help her and make her happy. We prayed for her constantly, and when our prayers weren't answered, it was difficult to see what good could come of this. We couldn't save Christina, but we didn't lose Aaron and Levi. Now we have you, and I count that a blessing."

Jade bit her lips and swallowed, unable to form words without opening the floodgates of her emotions. Aaron and Levi meant so much to her, and they'd suffered so much loss.

They didn't speak the rest of the ride to church. Slipping into the dimly lit sanctuary, they found their places with the family. Levi tapped

Jade's arm as she sat, pointing out how quiet he could be through the candlelight service.

She wrapped her arm around his shoulders and kissed his head, thankful for the boy sitting beside her and the man who rested his arm on the back of the pew to lay his hand on her shoulder.

When the invocation began, Jade and Mama Harding stood, making their way out of the church without disrupting the service. During the drive back to the ranch, Mama Harding listed off the things that still needed to be done before everyone arrived. Jade focused on her duties, determined to do her part to make the Christmas celebration joyous for everyone.

The women moved efficiently throughout the kitchen and meeting room, and when the family and guests arrived, everyone was ready to sit down to a feast.

When plates were filled, Jade took her place beside Levi and waited as Silas stood at the front of the grand room.

Silence fell over the tables as the patriarch of the Harding family prepared to ask the Lord's blessing of the food.

"Father, we thank You for the blessings You've laid before us tonight. Thank You for allowing the James and Burke families to be with us as we celebrate the birth of the Savior. We thank You for Your mighty sacrifice, and the forgiveness and grace You show us daily. Please bless this food and the hands that prepared it. In Jesus' name we pray. Amen."

A few whispers of "Amen" filled the room, and voices began to rise.

"Wait!" Camille stood with her hand raised. "I have something to say before we dig in." She brushed her dark hair over her shoulder and extended her hand to Noah, who stood from his seat beside her.

"We have so much to be thankful for. This family has grown so much this year, and we've made some wonderful friends." Her gaze cut to her husband, who watched her with a look of adoration similar to the one Aaron often gave Jade.

"But next year, we'll have even more family to love." Camille lifted the hand that was linked to Noah's and screamed, "We're having a baby!"

Hoots and whistles filled the room in an instant, and everyone rose from their seats.

"Wait!" Haley screamed above the noise. "Us too!" She slapped both hands over her mouth as her eyes grew wide.

More screams erupted as Asher cried, "You said I could tell!"

Levi jumped up and ran to Haley who was closest and wrapped his arms around her waist.

Jade turned to Aaron as tears filled her eyes. "We're having babies!"

The happy tears gushed so hard, she covered her eyes. Her shoulders shook with sobs as Aaron wrapped his strong arms around her.

"I'm so happy." Her words were murmured and choked as she buried her face in Aaron's chest.

Aaron rubbed circles on her back as she brushed tears from her face, and when she looked up at him, his green eyes were glowing with love.

Jade laughed. "I'm such a sap."

Shaking his head, Aaron whispered, "I love you."

"I love you too." She brushed her hands over her cheeks once more. "We should congratulate them."

When hugs had been sufficiently given, everyone returned to their seats to begin the meal. Jade didn't notice Hunter's absence until she'd nearly finished eating. Concerned, she turned to Aaron and jerked her head toward the empty seat.

He nodded and turned back to his plate without explanation. Hunter tended to exclude himself from many social activities, and she wasn't sure why. Aaron had told her how he'd gotten the jagged scar on his face. It seemed like a heroic tale—he'd been attacked by wild dogs while trying to protect Lucas when they were younger.

Without knowing more about Hunter, she couldn't understand why he distanced himself from the happiest moments. It wasn't her business, so she resolved to pray for him and the battle only the Lord knew.

After dinner, Asher and Haley led Christmas carols. Half an hour later, Silas and Mama Harding distributed gifts to everyone. Even the guests were thrilled to receive framed photos from their riding lessons at the ranch.

When the festivities began to wane, Levi had dark circles under his eyes and leaned on Jade's shoulder.

Aaron slid his hands under his son's arms and lifted him. "Come on. I think we've had enough fun for one day."

Surprisingly, Levi didn't protest and allowed his dad to carry him to the truck. Jade slid into the seat beside him, and Levi rested his head in her lap. She brushed her hands through his short hair and felt a thrill of excitement for the coming morning. Spending Christmas with the Hardings had been more than she'd expected.

Aaron parked the truck in front of her cabin and shut off the engine. Levi didn't stir in her lap.

"Merry Christmas," Aaron whispered.

"Merry Christmas. What time should I be ready in the morning?"

"I'll call when we wake up. Levi usually gets up earlier than normal, and we open presents at the main house before breakfast."

"Sounds good. Thanks for letting me spend the holiday here with your family."

Aaron brushed her hair behind her ear. "You're always welcome here. This is your home, and this is your family too."

Assurance filled her at Aaron's words. This did feel like home, and she desperately wanted to belong to this family. She loved her own, but how blessed would she be to have both?

"Thank you." She leaned over and gave him a quick kiss. "I love you."

"I love you too." He slid his hands under Levi and lifted him to rest on his shoulder. "Good night."

"Good night."

Chapter Nineteen

AARON

Aaron knocked on the door of Hunter's cabin just before twilight. It had been a week since Christmas, and Hunter had been more reclusive than normal.

Hunter opened the door seconds later. "Everything okay?"

"That depends. You hangin' in there?" Aaron asked.

Hunter crossed his arms over his chest. "Why wouldn't I be?"

"No reason. Just haven't seen your face much."

Hunter huffed. "Count it a blessing."

"Don't be a stranger. You know we don't care if you're ugly."

The comment earned a small twitch in Hunter's mouth. Aaron learned a long time ago that the only way to break through Hunter's defenses was to laugh at his expense.

"Thanks, man. Nothing is wrong. I'm just never gonna be the life of the party."

Hunter's parents had skipped out on him when he was still young, but the rest of the family did their best to make him feel included. Still, nothing seemed to ease that rigid exterior he put on every day.

"You playin' tonight?" Aaron asked.

"Yeah. I'm right behind you. Just need to grab a few things."

"See you later." He never knew if he was coming or going when it came to Hunter, but all Aaron could do was try. His cousin didn't deserve the weight he carried. The sins that pinned him down weren't his to bear.

Aaron walked over to Jade's cabin and knocked on the door. She answered within seconds, and an eager smile spread across her face.

"I'm ready," she said as she hoisted the strap of her purse on her shoulder.

"Your chariot awaits."

"Where's Levi?" she asked as she closed the cabin door behind her.

"Waiting in the car. He's been sitting on ready for an hour."

Jade chuckled and jogged to the truck. Aaron could breathe easier when Jade and Levi were happy, and everyone at the ranch was excited for the celebration tonight. Camille and Haley wanted to celebrate their pregnancy news on New Year's Eve with everyone at Barn Sour tonight. Haley had even created a playlist for Aaron and Hunter.

"Are you ready to party?" Jade asked Levi as she scooted into the seat beside him.

"I was born ready!" Levi screamed.

"Whoa, bud. We're all right here. No need to yell."

"Sorry. I'm just excited."

"Me too," Jade said. "You think you'll be able to stay up?"

"Oh, yeah. I'm a big boy."

Asher and Hunter were planning to stage a fake New Year's countdown at 8:00 so Levi could be there. Aaron had no plans to stay at Barn Sour any later than that. New Year's Eve in an establishment with an alcohol license wasn't on his list of things to do.

After supper, Asher and Hunter got the music going, and almost everyone moved to the dance floor. While Levi made his rounds dancing with every woman he knew, Aaron taught Jade the basics of the two-step.

"Is it bad that I'm enjoying teaching you something for a change?"

Jade laughed. "It was about time we switched things up. Looks like I'm going to need a lot of practice."

Aaron pulled her in close as Asher crooned the beginnings of a slow song. "Nah. You're doing great. You can't be good at everything."

She tilted her head as she looked up at him. Her blue eyes seemed darker in the dim light. "You're good at a lot of things I don't understand. I can't change a tire or the oil in my car."

Aaron leaned closer and brushed his cheek against hers to whisper, "Is that why you keep me around?"

She gasped low as he trailed kisses down her neck. Brushing her hair aside, he let his thumb trail down her neck. He felt her pulse drumming rapid and steady as he kissed his way back up to her jaw.

"Daddy!"

Aaron leaned away from Jade's tempting skin and scanned the room for his son. He'd gotten completely lost in the moment with Jade and forgot they were in a public place.

Levi barreled into Aaron's leg. "Uncle Asher said it's almost time. I need one of those horn things."

"Right. I think Laney has them. Let's find her." Keeping a hold on Jade's hand, they set off to find the party horns together.

Five minutes later, they all had party horns and New Year's hats when Asher stepped up to the mic. "Okay, folks. This is the junior countdown for the evening, so grab your kiddos and get ready to ring in the new year!"

Jade squeezed Aaron's hand, and he picked Levi up as Asher began the countdown from ten.

"Five, four, three, two, one!"

A chorus of "Happy New Year" rang through the building. Levi wrapped one arm around Aaron's neck and reached his other arm toward Jade. She pushed up onto her toes so Levi could include her in the hug.

Aaron tightened his hold on the people he loved. He had everything. He couldn't ask for anything better than this.

Levi blew the party horn only inches from Aaron's ear, and he squeezed his eyes shut tight as if closing them would plug his ears.

"Whoa. Too loud," Aaron said.

"Can I go blow it over there?" Levi asked.

Aaron set Levi on his feet and watched him run to blow the horn beside Maddie and Lucas.

When he turned back to Jade, she threw her arms around him and kissed him hard. How could he have forgotten the New Year's kiss?

She pulled back and said, "Sorry. I know it isn't officially midnight, but I might not make it that long."

Aaron kissed her again, dragging his lips over hers, drinking her in as if he couldn't get enough. It would never be enough. If he had the ring right now, he'd ask her to marry him without hesitation.

As he broke the kiss, he remembered the reason why he didn't have the ring yet. He wanted to wait until she got home from visiting her family. If she spent time with her grandparents and changed her mind about staying here, she would have a way out. As much as he wanted her to stay, he couldn't trap her in a life she wasn't completely sure she wanted.

Chapter Twenty

JADE

Levi sat in Jade's lap in the recliner as she read *The Giving Tree*. It was one of her favorite books for a number of reasons, and she hoped Levi understood the deeper meaning in the allegory of the tree.

Her phone vibrated in her back pocket as she neared the end of the book. She chose not to check the message right away. It was her favorite part of the story, and she was choking back tears. How could so few words have such a strong impact?

She closed the book and said, "The end."

"Another?" Levi asked.

"Hold on a second." She shifted Levi in her lap to wiggle the phone from her pocket.

It was a text from Aaron.

Aaron: I'm going to be late tonight. Can you put Levi to bed?

"It's your dad," Jade said. "It's going to be a late night, but he said it's time for you to go to bed."

Levi whined. "Just one more?"

"Go get ready for bed, and I'll read another when I come to tuck you in."

"Okay!" Levi took off for his bedroom to grab pajamas.

Resigned to settle in for the night, Jade opened her laptop to make notes about Levi's progress today. When the internet connected, her email notifications dinged.

She could check those first and then come back to her notes. Clicking to the inbox, one sender caught her eye. It was the Scottish job board, and the subject line was one she'd never received before.

We would like to request an interview.

She quickly scanned the first few lines of the email, her heart racing with each word she read. Before she finished reading, she grabbed the laptop and jumped to her feet. "No way!"

Levi threw open the door to his room. "What's happening?"

"I just... got a job interview." Her sentence trailed off as she realized the moment didn't hold the excitement she'd always thought it would.

Levi's eyes grew wide as he asked, "What does that mean?"

"It means—" She stopped, unable to tell Levi what it meant because she'd just realized it herself.

Getting the job meant leaving Blackwater.

"I—It means I've been considered for a job teaching kids in Scotland."

Levi tilted his head slightly. "You told me Scotland is a long way away."

Jade set the laptop on the couch and opened her arms. "It is, but—"

"You're leaving?" The tears came without warning, and the wails followed.

"Wait, no." She went to him, pulling him as close as she could without suffocating him. "Listen, you don't need to cry."

"I don't want you to leave," Levi said through tears.

She stroked a hand over his hair and whispered, "It's okay. I'm not leaving. Everything is okay." If he didn't stop crying soon, her own tears would come. She'd been so caught up in her own excitement she hadn't realized what she was doing. Now, she'd broken Levi's trust that she'd worked so hard to gain.

"Levi, please listen to me. I'm not leaving." She cupped his face in both of her hands and forced him to look at her. He fought hard to control the sniffles and sobs.

"I'm not leaving you. They asked for an interview, and yes, I *used* to want that job, but I don't want it more than I want you. Do you understand? You're first, and nothing can change that."

Levi nodded slowly, but the tears came fresh. She pulled him in tight and repeated the words, "I love you, Levi Bennett Harding."

"You got it right!" Levi said with a smile.

Soon, he was able to wipe the remaining tears from his face, and he straightened his shoulders.

"Are you sure?" he asked.

"I'm sure. I love you. My home is here with you."

Levi nodded again, seeming surer this time.

"Okay, now that we've settled that, let's get you to bed."

He threw his arms around her neck and hugged her again.

"I'll be right there to tuck you in."

"And read a book?" he asked.

"Yes. Which one do you want to read?"

"Let's read that one again."

"Sure."

Feeling horrible for hurting Levi's feelings, she tucked him in, read the story while shedding a few tears this time, and then took her usual seat on the couch where she read her Bible in the evenings when Aaron was late getting in.

The Bible rested in her lap, but she didn't open it. Instead of reading, she bowed her head and prayed—for guidance, peace, and understanding. She didn't yearn for the job in Scotland the way she had before. She loved teaching Levi, and she'd been teaching Sunday school for weeks now. She was happy here in a way she'd never known before, and she had no desire to leave. Yes, she planned to visit her grandparents soon, but that was temporary.

She was still praying when Aaron got home, and she stood as soon as she heard his footsteps on the porch.

She opened the door before he'd finished removing his boots, and the smile that greeted her dissolved all that was left of her indecision.

"Hey, beautiful."

Her mind was tired from worrying, and she couldn't force her body to move. There was no decision to make. The answer was right here in front of her, and the tension she'd been carrying fell from her shoulders.

She stood motionless in the doorway as Aaron cupped her face and slid his fingers into her hair. Tilting her head up, he kissed her jaw and her temple before capturing her mouth with his. The night around them was sharp and cold, but the blood in her veins ran like fire.

Her hands slid to his back, and she clung to him. This was her home. This was the man she loved.

When he broke the kiss, a low rumble sounded in his chest. "Have I told you lately that coming home to you is my favorite part of the day?"

"You have, but I wouldn't mind hearing it again."

He leaned down to hook his arms behind her knees and shoulders, lifting her into his arms in one fell swoop. "Then I'll just have to tell you every day. How's that?"

She laughed as he carried her inside. "I have no objections."

He laid her gently on the couch and dotted kisses all over her face. "How was Levi today?"

"Perfect. Did you know it's fifty-nine steps between my cabin and yours?"

"Let me guess, Levi counted."

"Of course. And he checked it twice."

Aaron stood and brushed a hand over his coat. "I'm filthy. I should get cleaned up."

Jade sat up on the couch. "I should get going too. I'll see you in the morning."

He kissed her at the door before she started for her cabin with her laptop bag hung over her shoulder. She hadn't worried over the email anymore, but she knew she'd send a reply tonight declining the offer. She loved her work, and she loved Scotland, but what would it cost to take that job? It would cost her everything she loved here in Blackwater.

She couldn't give up a life of love with a man and his son who cherished her to chase dreams.

Chapter Twenty-One

AARON

Aaron pushed open the door to Levi's room. The rising sun shone dimly through the transparent curtains over the small picture window in the middle of the wall and fell on Levi's chestnut-brown hair.

"Morning, bud. Up and at 'em."

Levi rolled over to face his dad. "Is it morning already?"

It wasn't like Levi to lie around even for a second once his eyes opened in the morning. "You feeling okay?"

"Yeah. I just didn't sleep a lot." He rubbed his eyes and sat up. The blanket and sheet fell into a heap in his lap.

Aaron stepped into the room and sat on the side of the bed. He rested the back of his hand on Levi's forehead. No fever. "What kept you up?"

Levi looked down at his hands. "I was worried."

"About what?" Aaron worked hard to give Levi a worry-free life. The kid had it made.

"Jade. She got all excited last night because she got some job she wanted, but it's in Scotland, and she told me that's a long, long, long way away."

Aaron froze. Everything grew quiet, and the only thing he could hear was his heart beating wildly and restlessly in his chest. "Are you sure?"

"Yeah. She said she wasn't going to take it, but I'm still scared. She was so excited about it. She won't leave though, will she?"

How could he say for certain that she wouldn't't? "I don't know for sure, but if she said she wouldn't, then I think we can trust her."

Could it be that simple? He trusted Jade with the most precious part of his life—his son—every day. Could he trust her to choose him when the opportunity she'd wanted for so long was handed to her?

"Okay. Then I'm fine. I just don't want her to go."

Aaron pulled his son in and hugged him tightly. "Me either. I love her too." He released the hug and patted Levi on the shoulder. They'd both need to be strong and prepared for anything in the days to come, and Aaron wouldn't have the luxury of moping around. He was still a parent and he was still a vital worker at the ranch. Life went on whether the woman he loved left them or not, so he'd have to put on a brave face for Levi.

***

The door to Jade's cabin opened before he put the truck in park, and she ran through the snow-dusted grass to hop into the passenger seat. "Good morning."

"Morning," Levi said as he wrapped her in his usual morning hug.

"Good morning," Aaron said, sounding much calmer than he felt. Jade hadn't mentioned the job when he'd come home last night, but she must have gotten word about it before Levi went to bed. Why hadn't she said anything?

Everything was completely ordinary through breakfast, except for Aaron's elevated blood pressure. Jade was her usual sweet self, and she didn't give one hint or say a single word that would lead him to believe she'd gotten a job offer. Maybe it was just a request for an interview. Would she have to appear in person for that, or would they allow her to interview virtually because of the distance?

He worried more during his morning duties. He'd earned a few extra cuts and bruises while working under the hood of a ranch truck. Distraction morphed into frustration before he stepped away and headed to the main house early for lunch. Maybe he could get Jade alone and ask her what was going on.

Jade and Levi weren't at the main house, and he fought the urge to go looking for them. The more anxious he got about talking to Jade, the worse the turmoil rolled in his middle. He'd never made himself sick with worry before, but he wondered if throwing up his guts would make him feel better at this point.

When she did show up for lunch, she had Levi as well as two other kids with her. She was smiling bright and joyful as usual, and the familiar happiness on her face relaxed his heart rate a fraction.

He tried to catch her attention after lunch, but the kids had already surrounded her.

She brushed a strand of hair that had fallen from her high ponytail as he approached. "Sorry. I promised them we could play on the obstacle course after lunch."

"No problem." Aaron pressed a soft kiss to her forehead and lingered. How many more days would he have to share with her? It made his heart sink to his toes to think their time together was coming to an end. He'd been imagining forever with her, but what if that weren't the reality? "I'll be home early tonight."

Jade waved a hand as a kid tugged her by her other hand toward the door. "You don't have to rush. I'm not going anywhere."

Aaron tried not to react to her words, but they twisted something inside him. Was he reading too much into what she said? A part of him wished Levi hadn't spilled the beans this morning. The whole day had been torture after the crippling news.

He pushed through the rest of the afternoon, throwing himself into his workload to keep his mind on anything except Jade.

At supper, he stayed glued to Jade's side. Maybe if they didn't talk about it, he could pretend things weren't about to change. How could she be so calm when he was getting ulcers worrying in silence?

When Jade stood to take her empty plate to the serving bar, Aaron followed her.

"Hey, is Levi caught up on his lessons?" he asked.

"Yep. We finished this morning. He was eager to play with the other kids."

"Good. Do you have plans tonight? I was wondering if you'd like to watch a movie with us."

She nodded emphatically. "That sounds great. I definitely don't have plans. Are you finished working for the day?"

Aaron placed his plate on the serving counter beside Jade's. "I finished. I just need to get my orders for tomorrow, and I'll be free."

"Great. Any certain movie you want to watch, or should I let Levi pick?"

"Let him pick. He doesn't get to watch TV often."

Jade kissed Aaron's cheek, and he wrapped his arm around her waist, wishing he could hold her like this forever.

Aaron listened as Micah rattled off the duties for tomorrow. It wasn't a heavy load. Maybe Aaron would be able to cut out early again. If he didn't have much time left with Jade, he wanted to make sure he spent as much of it with her as possible.

He joined Jade and Levi in the living room at the main house half an hour later. The cabins didn't have TV, so the main house was the hub for local news and weather forecasts as well as old-fashioned DVDs his mother picked up from the library sales in town.

Levi jumped from the couch where he sat beside Jade. "I picked *The Sword in the Stone*!"

Aaron held out his fist to Levi who bumped it with his own. "Good choice." It was one of Aaron's old favorites. He could have been stuck with *The Lion King*. That was one he couldn't stomach.

He settled onto the couch beside Jade and rested his arm on the back of the couch. When Levi fell asleep, she turned to Aaron and cuddled closer in his arms. He wasn't sure why they kept watching the movie without speaking, but he drank in the peace of the moment while it lasted.

When the movie was over, Jade reached to turn the TV off.

Aaron rested a hand on her arm. "Hey, can we talk?"

Concern flashed in her features as she said, "Of course. In the office?"

Aaron nodded. She laid a blanket over Levi and led the way to the office in the back of the house. He stepped inside and closed the door behind them. If Levi woke up, he'd go to the kitchen first and find Mama Harding.

"What's wrong?" she asked.

He didn't answer her at first. He wasn't sure he could look at her for this conversation, so he took the coward's way out and wrapped her in his arms. The smell of her hair reminded him of the mark she'd left on his home and in his life. Being in this room with her brought back memories of the day they'd met and she'd changed his life forever.

After trying to catch his breath and failing, he said, "Levi told me about the job."

Her arms tightened around his back. "Aaron—"

"Wait. I've been tied up in knots all day trying to forget about it, but I can't dance around it anymore. I want you to know I love you, but I know this is what you've wanted your whole life. It's a great opportunity, and I know you're the best person for the job." He tightened his hold on her and swallowed the lump in his throat.

She pulled back slightly, but he held on and continued.

"I love you, and I'll always love you. I would do it all again. Even knowing I'd have to watch you walk away, I'd fall in love with you all over again. Every time."

She shook her head and pushed him away. "Stop. It was just an interview, but I turned it down."

Her words were muffled as if he were hearing them underwater. "What?"

"I'm not going," she repeated.

"You're not?"

She stepped closer and kept her gaze locked on him. "I love you, and I'm not going anywhere." Her soft fingertips brushed his temple and slid down to cup his jaw.

He couldn't wait any longer. He crushed his lips to hers and drank her in. He'd been torturing himself all day, but this was why she hadn't told him. She really wasn't going. She'd already turned down the interview. It didn't matter whether she'd told him about the offer or not if it wasn't standing between them.

Her fingernails dug into his back as she pulled him closer, desperate for the assurance they both needed. She was here, and he wasn't losing her.

When she pulled away, she touched her lips, and her hand was shaking. "I'm sorry I didn't tell you. I didn't want you to worry, but I guess you did that anyway."

Aaron shook his head. "It doesn't matter. I should have known you'd tell me if you planned to go." He looked at his feet, ashamed of the way he'd reacted all day. "Plus, Levi told me you weren't going, but it was hard to believe him. I know how much you want that job."

"I *wanted* that job. I don't anymore. I've wanted to go for so long, I didn't know what it felt like to want to stay until I met you and Levi."

Aaron's jaw tensed beneath her hand. "I'm afraid you'll regret it if you don't go."

She shook her head and smiled. "I won't. I'm happy here, and I know I would regret leaving you and Levi. I can't go."

He wrapped her in his arms, and she rested her head on his chest. The weight of the day dissolved, leaving only peace.

"I did book a flight to visit my grandparents," she said.

"That's good. I know you miss them."

"I wish you and Levi could go with me."

He rubbed circles on her back. "We don't have passports, but we'll get them. I'd like to go with you next time."

She raised her head and smiled. "I'd love that. I've talked about you and Levi so much, Gran is eager to meet you."

Thoughts he'd never expected popped into his mind. If he proposed and she said yes, would her grandparents be able to come to the wedding? She would want them to be there, but she said they were older and unsure about flying such a long way.

"I can't wait to meet her too. I bet Levi will love her."

"Oh, definitely. She loves the stories I tell her about him."

He hugged her close again. "I love you."

"I love you too," she whispered. "I'll hurry back."

Chapter Twenty-Two

JADE

In the weeks leading up to her trip to Scotland, Jade tried to make sure things would run as smoothly as possible at the ranch in her absence. Levi was caught up on his lessons, and she'd gone over a few things he could work on with Camille and Haley if they got the chance.

Aaron had asked if Levi could take a break from school, and she agreed. He was always working ahead, and they could shift his spring vacation to February. Aaron wanted to keep Levi with him on the ranch during the days, hoping it would help keep his mind off Jade.

Her flight would be leaving at noon from Billings Logan International Airport, and Levi refused to be left behind. Jade opted to sit in the backseat of Micah's truck on the drive. Aaron's older model truck only had a bench seat, and Levi needed a car seat to ride anywhere off the ranch.

Levi fell asleep twenty minutes into the trip, but he held his grip on her hand. She'd booked a flight back in only six days because she'd been reluctant to leave him for any longer.

Holding Levi's small hand in hers, she prayed most of the drive to the airport. Leaving them was a tough decision, but hopefully they'd be able to come with her next time. She wouldn't have insisted on the trip if her grandparents were in better health. They gave her updates when she asked, but she liked to see for herself how they were doing. Not that she could do much, but she planned to help out at the restaurant while she visited.

When they arrived at the airport, Aaron entered the parking deck.

"Are you parking? I thought you would just drop me off."

"Not a chance. I'm walking you inside. You actually thought I would dump you out at the curb?"

She grinned as his gaze met hers in the rear-view mirror. "Maybe. You might be ready to get rid of me."

"I'm not kicking you to the curb just yet." Levi's hand gripped hers tighter. "No. Don't leave yet. Daddy said we could say good-bye inside."

She patted his hand. "That's true. We haven't parked yet."

Levi kept his hold on her hand while Aaron tugged her suitcase and carry-on. They stood to the side as she checked her bags and got her boarding pass. When they reached the security line, she crouched next to Levi. "I have to go the rest of the way on my own now." She hugged him tight and whispered, "One, four, three."

"One, four, three," he whispered back.

"I'll be back before you know I'm gone."

Levi released his arms from around her neck. "Do you have the rock?"

She reached into her pocket and pulled out the rock he'd given her when she'd first showed up at Blackwater Ranch. "Always."

"You won't forget me?" he asked with a quiver in his voice.

"I could never forget you. I don't need a rock to remind me, either. You're on my mind all the time."

Levi looked down at his shoes and said, "I don't know why we have to miss people."

She wanted to be strong in front of Levi, but he shattered every wall around her heart, leaving a tear spilling from her eye. "We don't have to miss people if we carry them in our hearts."

Levi rested his hand on his chest. "Then I'll keep you right here."

She hugged him again and wiped the tear from her cheek. "You're so brave. I'll video chat with you every day. How does that sound?"

Levi nodded vigorously.

She stood and looked to Aaron and fought the tears again. "It's only for a week," she said, and the sobs followed.

His arms were around her, and her face was buried in his chest. She loved being this close to him. She could smell the woodsy soap he used, and she begged her mind to remember every little thing about him. She wouldn't be gone long enough to get used to the time change, and she knew there were many restless nights in her future. She didn't want to spend them missing Aaron and Levi so much her chest ached.

She lifted her head and Aaron kissed her sweetly until Levi gave an exaggerated gag beside them. Thankful he'd broken the sadness of the moment, she ruffled his hair. "I'll see you soon."

Aaron squeezed her hand, pulling her attention to him in the bustling airport. "I love you."

"I love you too. I'll call or text during every layover." She had a long trip ahead of her, but this was the first time she'd dreaded the travel. She'd seen dozens of airports, since her family flew to Scotland almost every summer and Christmas.

She kissed Levi's head as she moved to get in line for the security screening and waved one last good-bye as she walked around a corner and out of sight.

She'd expected this to be difficult, but she wasn't prepared for the emotional upheaval today would bring. She'd be back in Blackwater in only a few days. At least it wasn't a two-week visit like she normally planned when she made the twenty-plus-hour trip around the world.

Once she'd made it to her assigned seat on the plane, she settled in with a paperback book she'd picked up at a store in the airport. She'd barely gotten interested in chapter one when her thoughts drifted to the wedding magazine she'd impulsively purchased at the same time as the book. She promised herself she would scan it and throw it away before landing in Inverness. While she loved dreaming about planning a wedding, she didn't want to get her family's hopes up, or better yet, her own. Aaron hadn't hinted at marriage yet, but he assured her on numerous occasions that he was committed to their relationship.

Just after takeoff, she quietly slipped the magazine from her bag. The cover model wore a beautiful dress with lacework down the back and a small train that fanned out around her.

"You getting married?" the woman beside her asked. She had a slight northeastern accent, and her hair reminded Jade of the auburn color of fall.

"Oh, not yet. I mean, I'm seeing someone, but he hasn't asked me yet."

"Are you on your way to see him?"

Jade closed the magazine. "No, actually, I just left him. I'm on my way to visit my grandparents."

The woman hummed. "Absence makes the heart grow fonder."

"That's the truth. I didn't want to leave him."

The woman patted Jade's hand. It was such a motherly gesture, and it reminded Jade that she'd forgotten to call her mom before the plane took off.

"I wish you both the best. Where are you headed?"

The word had been on the tip of her tongue before she bit it back. *Home.*

But she wasn't headed home. She was leaving her home. "Scotland. You?"

"Boston. Visiting my grandkids."

Jade smiled. Perhaps chatting with a kind stranger would take her mind off leaving.

***

Twenty-three hours later, she stepped off the small plane at Inverness Airport. The February wind was freezing, and she tugged her wool-lined coat tighter around her. The walk into the airport from where the plane landed was a few hundred yards, and she hitched her carry-on higher on her shoulder as she walked.

The flight hadn't been full, but half an hour had passed before her bag slowly crept down the baggage carousel. She texted her grandparents, who were waiting for her in a nearby parking lot. She'd have to get used to calling it a car park again. She adored the simple differences in the language between America and Scotland. It was nice to mix things up a bit.

She spotted her grandparents' vehicle as she exited the building. Thankfully, she didn't have to wait outside in the cold. Her grandparents stepped out of the car at the same time. Gran wrapped her in a hug first while Pop loaded her bags.

They all shuffled into the car quickly to get out of the cold highland air, and they talked for a few minutes before Jade's head became heavy. She forgot how hard it was to make the whole flight in one day, and she made a mental note to split up the flight into two days if Aaron and Levi traveled with her next time.

It was still early morning in Fort Augustus when they arrived at her grandparents' house. Their workday was about to begin, and she was ready to fall into bed and sleep for a week.

"We'll be leaving soon, and you'll have time to catch up on some sleep," her grandmother said as they stepped into the entryway.

"I think I'm going to try to power through. I just need a few minutes to brush my teeth and let everyone know I made it safely."

"If you insist," Gran said as she stepped out of the way so Pop could carry the heavier bag up to the guest room.

Jade thanked him with a hug and promised to meet him downstairs in half an hour, but when the door closed, she fell face-first onto the bed.

Rolling over onto her back, she checked her messages and replied to everyone, including her mother, her sister, and Aaron, letting them know she'd arrived safely. She added an extra line in Aaron's message promising to call later since everyone on the other side of the world was still sleeping.

After responding to messages, she opened her email. There were a few messages waiting, but they'd have to wait a little longer. She couldn't keep her eyes open to read them, much less respond.

She jumped out of bed, brushed her teeth, and did a few jumping jacks to get her blood flowing before trudging downstairs to meet her grandparents. She'd grab a cup of coffee at The Four Winds.

Gran was tying a scarf around her neck near the entryway.

"Where's Pop?" Jade asked as she grabbed her own scarf from the coat rack.

"He left a few minutes ago. You know him. Always early."

Jade followed Gran out the door. "You didn't have to wait for me. I know the way." The Four Winds was only a few steps from the house, and her Pop only came home to sleep.

"You really should consider taking a nap," her grandmother said.

"I'll leave early. I'll make it as long as I can. I'm just so excited to see you. I didn't come all this way just to sleep."

The restaurant was beginning to stir with guests by the time Jade and her grandmother arrived. She even recognized a few faces.

The day was long but filled with smiles and pleasant chatter. The high tourist season wouldn't begin for a few months, and the slower pace did nothing to keep her exhaustion at bay.

Just after the lunch rush, Jade rested her chin in her hands and propped her elbows on the checkout counter.

"You ready to call it a day?" Pop asked.

"I think so. I can't keep my eyes open."

"Go on home," he patted her shoulder. "You'll feel better in the morning."

She said her good-byes to Gran with a promise to join them for breakfast in the morning. Her feet felt heavy as she walked to her grandparents' house, and she shed her thick outer clothing in a daze as soon as she stepped inside.

In her room, she fell onto the bed and pressed Aaron's contact on the messenger app they could use internationally. She hoped Levi was with him so she could say hello to both of them.

Levi answered the phone. "Jade! I miss you!"

"I miss you too, bud. You taking care of Daddy?"

"Sure am. We're changin' the tires on Uncle Noah's truck. He ran over a hole in the north pasture and dented his rim!"

Jade closed her eyes. "I'm sure you'll get it all fixed up."

There was a shuffling on the line, and Aaron's deep voice greeted her. "Hey, beautiful."

She was too tired to respond with anything more than a lazy, "Hey."

"You about to crash?" he asked.

"Mhmm," she hummed.

"We'll talk to you tomorrow. Get some rest."

"Okay. Love you." She didn't have an ounce of strength left, and she was fading fast.

"We love you," were the last words she heard before she fell asleep.

Chapter Twenty-Three

AARON

Jade had been gone four days, and Aaron hadn't worked up the courage to wipe her message off the bathroom mirror in his cabin. She'd scribbled the numbers "1, 4, 3," on the mirror in pink lipstick the morning they'd driven her to the airport.

Aaron liked it, and so did Levi. So they'd both be staring at her numbers every morning and evening while they brushed their teeth.

Aaron pulled a T-shirt on and turned away from the message on the mirror. He shouldn't need the reminder. She was coming back in a few days, and she'd called every evening like clockwork.

In the kitchen, Levi had poured a bag of Skittles onto the round, wooden table and sorted them into piles by color.

"Look! Red has the most and green has the least," Levi said.

"Step away from the sugar pills. You haven't had breakfast yet."

Levi groaned. "We can't leave yet. Jade hasn't called."

"She will any minute now. No whining." He'd been doing a lot of whining lately, and Aaron assumed it was because he missed Jade. The schedule she'd made and followed with Levi every day had been thrown into chaos this week.

Aaron's phone rang on the kitchen counter, and Levi almost tipped the chair on its side in his scramble to get to it.

"Hello," Levi said as he answered and pressed the phone to his ear.

"Put it on speaker," Aaron said.

Levi held the phone out and pressed the button. "What are you doing?"

"Just helping out at my grandparents' restaurant. What do you and Daddy have planned today?"

"We're going fishing! Uncle Lucas is going too."

"That sounds like fun! Will you take me when I get back?" she asked.

"Sure will. Yesterday, I did the obstacle course twenty-five times!"

"Wow. Did you fall asleep early after all that?"

"Yeah. Daddy had to carry me to bed."

Jade sighed. "I miss you so much."

"I miss you too. But it's almost time for you to come back!"

There was a pause before Jade said, "I have to go. We have a few customers right now, but can you ask your daddy to call me in about half an hour?"

"Sure," Aaron said. "Sorry. I've been here the whole time. I was just waiting my turn."

"Hey. It's good to hear your voice." There was a hint of something in her tone that he couldn't put his finger on. Unease? Exhaustion? She wasn't as upbeat as usual.

"I'll call you back," Aaron said.

"Thanks. Love you, Levi. Love you, Aaron."

"We love you too!" Levi screamed.

Aaron disconnected the call and shoved his phone in the back pocket of his jeans. "Let's load up. I think I heard Mama Harding say she was making pancakes for you."

"Yes!" Levi screamed as he darted for the door.

"Hold up. You need another layer," Aaron shouted.

Levi grabbed his coat off the rack, and Aaron was right behind him, buttoning his flannel shirt first, then slipping on his corduroy coat on top.

The snow was thick this morning, and he hoped Jade's flight wouldn't be delayed. He knew next to nothing about how flights worked in heavy snow conditions. He hadn't even been on a plane before. Dropping Jade off last week was the first time he'd ever set foot in an airport.

Jade, on the other hand, was a seasoned traveler. She'd told him stories about traveling through Western Europe and attending college in Glasgow and Atlanta. She'd even spent a summer taking college courses in Barcelona.

At the main house for breakfast, Levi fell into the serving line with Laney while Aaron excused himself to the living room to call Jade in private. Most of their conversations included Levi, and as much as Aaron loved his son's excitement to talk to Jade, he'd perked up at her request that he call her back.

He sat in the middle of the couch and leaned his elbows on his knees as he made the call. She answered on the second ring.

"Hey. I hope you're not busy," she said.

"Nah. It's breakfast time here, so no one noticed when I slipped out."

Jade sighed. "I actually had something I wanted to talk to you about."

Aaron rubbed his chin and tried not to assume the worst. "I'm all yours."

"The day before yesterday, I got another email from the headteacher that requested the interview before I came here. I actually didn't check it for a few days. I got completely off my schedule, and the jet lag was horrible. Anyway, she asked if she could call me to discuss some things. I said yes, not knowing what she might possibly want."

Jade always spoke fast when she was nervous, and her words were starting to run together. Aaron, on the other hand, couldn't catch his breath for a different reason.

"So, I called her. She said the position I applied for still hadn't been filled, and they were having trouble getting anyone else to even consider the position. The school is small. They only have one classroom for students in p1 through p7."

"What does that mean?" he asked, trying to delay the bad news he felt rushing toward him.

"It means the headteacher has to teach all ages. There just aren't enough students to justify individual classes by grade."

Aaron stared at a knot in the wood of the nearby coffee table. "Okay."

Jade sighed deep again. "She asked me to step in as a temporary instructor until they could fill the position. They have someone from the Edinburgh area who is willing to travel, but they need to find a replacement for her current position first. It's all just a mess, but really, it should be two weeks tops."

"So, you're staying?" he asked. He already knew the answer, but apparently, he was a glutton for punishment today.

"I don't know. I told her I needed time to think about it and talk it over with you. You're my boss and my boyfriend, and it's my job to teach Levi too."

"But these kids need you," Aaron said. He rested his forehead in his hand. "I know they're in a bind, and you can help them. It's not like you to walk away."

"It's not," Jade said with a sniffle. "I promise. I turned down the job. I don't want to stay here. I want to come home to you and Levi—"

"Hey, calm down," he said in the most soothing voice he could muster. He'd never been the placating kind, but he needed Jade to stop crying before his heart ripped in two. "We can work through this. I trust you. If you need to stay and help those kids out, we can manage here. I'm sure Haley or Laney can help me with Levi's lessons for a few weeks." He spit out the solutions as quickly as he could think. There was a problem, and he needed to solve it. Jade couldn't be unhappy. It made him sick to his stomach to think she was worrying about this decision.

"I'm sorry. I promise I didn't plan to stay. This is all new, and while I want to tell her I can't be the one to help her, I feel bad about it."

"I know," Aaron said, stopping her words that were barreling out like a freight train. "I understand. I know this is hard for you." He closed his eyes and said the words he needed to say, the ones he should say, for Jade and the students who didn't have a teacher. "But I know your heart, and if you're worried I won't trust you, you can forget that. This is what you always wanted to do, and you have a chance to do it. You get to have both. You can teach there knowing you're doing exactly what you always set out to do; teach a small group of kids where your family lives. But when they find someone in a few weeks, you can come back home."

He really hoped she heard that last part because, as much as he wanted her to do this, he selfishly hoped she would still want to come back to him when the time came. He might be sealing the fate of their relationship by encouraging her to do this, but he also couldn't beg her to come back to him knowing she would be unhappy.

"I still don't know," she said.

"Pray about it. Take the day to talk to your grandparents, your parents, and your sister. And know that it's okay if you don't get on a plane in two days."

"I will. I'll definitely keep praying about it." She sniffled. "I feel better after talking to you. I haven't made a decision yet, but knowing you're not upset with me is just—"

"And Jade," he whispered. "It's okay if you don't want to come back." The air left his lungs, and his mouth felt dry. He hated everything about this, but what choice did he have?

"That's not an option," she said, resolute.

"You might change your mind tomorrow."

"No. I won't change my mind about you, and that makes all the difference. I'm not lost. At least, I'm not anymore. I know the way home now. You're my home."

It hurt. The ripping in his chest reminded him how much he'd missed her these last few days. Knowing he'd have to wait even longer could have ripped him open, but he'd do it over and over for Jade. He'd do anything for her. He'd even talk to his parents to see if they could manage without him here. Because if it came down to it and Jade really wanted to teach in Scotland, he'd try his best to go to her so she wouldn't have to miss out. Levi would love it, and Aaron would do whatever he could to find work wherever she ended up.

"I love you," she said, enunciating each word. "I love you, and I'm not staying here forever. No matter what."

"I love you too." He did, and that made all the difference. Jade didn't want to leave, and he wanted her back in his arms.

He could wait two weeks for forever, and he could hold onto the ring he'd bought a little longer, but getting Levi to keep his mouth shut was going to be a different story.

Chapter Twenty-Four

JADE

Jade opened her messenger bag and started filling it with things on her desk. She wiggled things around until the books she'd read to the p1 students, the spelling tests for the p3 students, and the laptop the school system had loaned her fit neatly inside.

Henry was the only student left in the classroom, and he dried his hands at the sink where he'd been rinsing glasses from their colored celery experiment. "Is there anything else I can help with, Ms. Smith?"

"No, but thank you." Henry was one of the oldest students, and he always helped out with the younger children. With all ages in one class, it felt more like a family than a schoolroom.

"I'll see you tomorrow," he said on his way out.

"Have a wonderful evening." Jade hitched her bag onto her shoulder and made one last sweep of the room. Everything was perfectly back in order after the long day.

Though her workday was over, she still had an hour drive back to Fort Augustus. Two weeks in the Highlands hadn't been enough time to get used to the time change, and she often turned the volume on the radio higher on her drive home. She'd hopefully gather some energy after eating a warm dinner at The Four Winds.

Back at her grandparents' house, she stowed her messenger bag by the small writing desk and headed to the restaurant. She had at least an hour of prep work ahead of her this evening, but she needed the walk to the restaurant and a big supper to recharge.

Her grandmother greeted her with a smile at the entrance. "How was your day?"

"Wonderful," she said as she slipped into a chair at a nearby table. "I love these kids."

"You always have. Any news from the headteacher?"

Jade massaged her temples. She'd been so busy lately that she often forgot to drink enough water. Headaches had been a nightly occurrence since she arrived. "I don't believe so. I'll check my messages when I leave here."

"What can I get you from the kitchen?" Gran asked.

"I'd really love a shepherd's pie." Her eyelids were getting heavy, so she stood and grabbed a cup from the small nook just inside the kitchen before filling it with ice water. "How was your day?"

"Lovely as usual," her grandmother said. The sweetness of her voice was the same as it had been when Jade was younger. "Why don't I pack up the shepherd's pie? You look like you might fall asleep at the table."

Jade hummed in her throat. "That does sound like a good idea. I may take a short nap before I prepare for tomorrow's class."

Within minutes, Jade had a to-go box containing a hot meal, and she poured the water she'd been drinking into a carryout cup.

"I'll see you at home." Jade waved with a finger as she stepped out the door.

The weather was chilly as she walked back to her grandparents' house. Wyoming winters were harsher than in Scotland, and while she preferred the moderate weather here, she'd much rather be cuddled up by the fireplace with Aaron and Levi.

Jade left the food on the dining room table and trudged up the stairs to retrieve her laptop. She could respond to emails while she ate.

When she settled down with her food and her work, she read an email from the headteacher confirming the replacement teacher transfer to begin a week from today.

In her excitement, she called Aaron to tell him the good news.

When the call connected, she could hear the wind muffling Aaron's end of the call.

"Hello."

"Hey. You busy?"

"Never too busy for you. How was your day?"

She relaxed into the wooden chair and closed her eyes. "Long. I don't know how you do physical labor all day every day. I'm exhausted after sitting in a classroom."

"It's the time change," Aaron assured her.

"I know, but I have good news." She sat up straighter and pulled up the email.

"Lay it on me," Aaron said.

"My temporary placement ends a week from today."

Aaron whistled loud and hooted. "That's what I'm talkin' about."

"What? Tell me!" she heard Levi's muffled words on the line.

"Jade's coming home in a week," Aaron said.

"Woo hoo!" Levi shouted. "I want to talk to her."

"Hold on," Aaron said as he passed the phone to his son.

"Jade! I miss you," Levi said in greeting.

"I miss you too! I'll be home soon."

"I have a surprise for you. Daddy said—"

"And that's enough," Aaron said, taking the phone back from his son. "He's a terrible accomplice."

"Now, what was he saying about a surprise?" Jade asked.

"Nothing. You'll have to wait a week. Have you booked a flight?"

"Oh, I'm so glad you said that. I need to call the airline now."

"Yes. Please choose the fastest way home. I'll pay for the up-charge."

Jade laughed. "What if the fastest way home is in first class?" she joked.

"Do it. Put it on my card. You deserve a comfortable trip home."

Jade bit her lip and tried to get a handle on her whirling emotions. She would never take him up on the offer, but it was kind of him to suggest. "You're the best," she whispered.

"I love you."

"I love you too. I'll call you tomorrow."

With whispered good-byes, she disconnected the call and looked back at the email. One week and she would be back home in Blackwater. She'd enjoyed teaching here these last couple of weeks. And while it had been everything she'd ever dreamed it would be, she knew her future was in Wyoming. She'd found her home, and she couldn't wait to get back to the man and the boy who held her heart.

Chapter Twenty-Five

AARON

Aaron tucked his flannel shirt into his jeans as he scanned the cabin for his phone. Did he leave it at the main house? He didn't want to run back up there unless he had to. Levi wasn't happy about getting left behind to pick up Jade at the airport, and they'd have to replay the whole why and why not again.

Aaron wanted to spend the drive back with Jade alone. They were hardly ever alone without Levi, and as much as Aaron loved his son, he was going to be selfish with her first hours back in the States.

Plus, Levi would get to be a part of her big surprise. Aaron had convinced Levi he needed to be here getting things ready.

He'd just stepped into his bedroom to search for the phone when he heard it ringing in the living room. Following the tune, he picked it up and stuck it between his shoulder and ear as he finished buckling his belt. It was Jade.

"Hey. I'm walking out the door right now."

"About that," Jade said, drawing out her words in a stall that froze him in his tracks.

"What?"

"I have bad news," she said with a huff at the end.

"No. No. Don't say it."

"My flight was delayed."

"I said don't say it! Where are you? I'm on my way."

"I'm in Denver."

Aaron grabbed his coat off the rack as he headed out the door. "Denver it is. I'll see you in seven hours."

Jade laughed, and he heard a loud voice on her end of the call asking the passengers to fasten their seatbelts, move their seats to the upright position, and turn off all electronic devices. "Easy, cowboy. I'm kidding. We're taking off in Denver."

Aaron rolled his head from one side to the other, stretching his neck. "That was an awful joke. My patience has taken the day off."

"Sorry, I know you're as ready for me to be home as I am."

Aaron slid into the truck and closed the door. "I love you. Come to me as fast as you can."

"I'm running. I love you."

"Love you too."

He tossed the phone into the passenger seat and rested his forehead on the steering wheel. "Lord, please bring her home safely."

***

Jade talked the entire drive back to the ranch. He wasn't complaining. He loved her voice, and she had some great stories to tell about the students and her grandparents. After missing her for weeks, he'd happily sit quietly while she talked to her heart's content.

It also kept him from being tempted to spill the beans about her surprise. There were actually a number of surprises, so the less he talked, the better.

Jade bounced in her seat as they turned onto the drive leading to the ranch. "I'm so happy to be back. Fair warning, I might crash early tonight. I'm exhausted."

"Let's take your stuff to your cabin first and you can decide if you want to go to the main house for supper or if you want me to just bring you a plate."

"Oh, no. I want to see everyone tonight. I've missed them."

Aaron tried not to let on that her suggestion worked perfectly for his plan.

He carried the bags to her bedroom and set them down against the wall. In the living room, Jade stretched her arms to the ceiling and yawned.

"You ready to go?"

Aaron shook his head and slid his hands around her lower back, gently tugging her closer. "Not yet."

Unable to wait any longer, he pressed his lips to hers and let the vise around his chest slip away. Jade was home, and she was back in his arms where he hoped she'd always stay.

When they broke the kiss, she smiled up at him with her eyes still closed. "I missed you."

"I missed you too. I have a few things to talk to you about."

"Lay it on me," she said, lazily opening her light-blue eyes.

"I don't want to be your boss anymore."

Her smile fell, and she leaned back an inch. "What?"

Brushing a finger along her jaw, he studied the curve of her neck and the slight thrum of her pulse just below her skin. "I know I didn't handle you leaving very well. I was terrified the entire time you were gone. But the truth is, I needed you to leave."

"Um, okay," she mumbled.

"It forced me to move past those old insecurities. The nagging voice in the back of my mind that said I wasn't worth sticking around for."

"Aaron—"

He interrupted her with a gentle finger on her lips. "That was my problem. Not yours. I trusted you, and that was something I hadn't done in years. When you said you were coming back, I believed you. It took me a while to get comfortable enough to do that, but I did."

Her grin lifted again but fell just as quickly. "What does that have to do with you being my boss?"

"Do you have your laptop?" he asked.

Jade looked around. "Yes. It's in my carry-on." She moved out of his arms and disappeared into her bedroom, returning seconds later with the computer.

"Turn it on and go to the ranch website."

Jade sat down on the couch and typed in the site address. "Okay." Aaron sat beside her and pointed to the newest page tab. "Click that one."

"Children's Program?" she asked as she turned to him. "What's that?"

Aaron pointed to the screen. "Click it and see."

The page opened to a photo of Levi standing atop a round bale of hay surrounded by dozens of other bales.

"What?" she asked. Her pitch was higher as she scrolled down to find a list of activities.

"Haley added this page for you. We want to offer you a job as Children's Events Director."

"What?" Jade screamed. Her eyes were wide, and her mouth hung open for a moment before she clapped her hands over it.

Her eyes scanned the page. It was filled with photos of kids on the obstacle course, Levi holding up a fish he caught, and a young girl petting the newest horse, Goldie, with Maddie at their side.

"This is so cool! A hay maze!"

"We put it together last week. Levi loves it."

"It's amazing!"

"That's what I thought you'd say." Aaron picked up her hand and rested it in both of his. "We want this to be a place where families can visit and see what we do around here. But now that Jameson is helping out more, we can offer more trail rides for the adults, and it's hard to plan those things when they have kids with them. God gave you a gift for teaching children, and we want you to be able to do more of that here."

"Wow." Her eyes were still wide and staring at the screen. "I can't believe it."

"That brings me to your job teaching Levi."

Jade's attention jerked back to Aaron. "I still want to teach Levi."

"And you can," Aaron added. "The kids' program won't always be full-time hours. I think you could still teach Levi if that's what we decide."

"We?" Jade tilted her head to the side.

Still holding her hand in his, Aaron moved to kneel beside the couch.

Jade gasped as she realized what he was doing.

"Jade Smith, I want to live my life beside you. Levi and I applied for passports while you were gone, and in about four weeks we should be able to go almost anywhere in the world with you. I don't care where we are as long as we're together. The next time you go to see your family, I want to go too."

Jade bit her lips and nodded. A tear slid down her cheek as she whispered, "Okay."

Aaron's heart was beating hard against his chest as he asked, "Will you marry me?"

"Yes," Jade blurted. She pushed the computer to the side and threw her arms around his neck.

He held her, thanking God for sending Jade into his life.

A few moments later, he groaned. "So, I don't have the ring."

"It's okay. I don't need one," she said.

"Well, it's not that. I have a ring, but I just don't have it with me. Levi has it."

She pulled away with a shocked look on her face. "You gave it to Levi! Are you sure he won't lose it?"

Aaron rubbed the back of his neck. "I'm pretty sure. I actually told him I would wait till supper to ask you, and he wanted to hold onto it until then."

"You didn't!"

"I know, but I couldn't wait any longer to ask you. Any chance you'd let me propose again and act surprised?"

Jade threw her head back and laughed. "Two proposals in one day?"

"It's for a good cause," he said, wrapping his hands around her waist.

"I'll choose you twice today and every day from now on."

Aaron kissed her hard this time. Every instinct told him to pull her closer, love her deeper, and adore her again and again. He would choose her every day too, and forever started right now.

Chapter Twenty-Six

JADE

Aaron laid his hand on the doorknob of the main house and turned to Jade. "Ready?"

"Ready." She'd never been surer of anything in her life. Saying yes to Aaron once was amazing. Saying yes twice was fun. She couldn't wait to see Levi's face.

Aaron kissed her quickly before he opened the door. The meeting room was bright and bustling with suppertime chatting and laughter.

Haley was the first to spot them. "She's back!"

Levi's head popped up, and he jumped from his seat. "Jade!" He ran around the table and straight into her arms.

Jade crouched to his level and held him tight. She'd been dreaming about having Levi back in her arms for weeks, but this moment blew all of her imaginings out of the water. "Hey, bud. I missed you," she whispered.

"I missed you too." He released her from the welcome hug. "We have surprises for you!"

"Yay! I love surprises."

Levi held up a finger. "I'll be right back." He started to run off, then he turned back to his dad. "Is it time?"

Jade stood as Aaron nodded. Levi ran into the kitchen.

"I can't imagine what he could be looking for in the kitchen," she said. Did he really stash the ring in there?

Aaron rubbed the back of his neck and shrugged. "Beats me."

Levi reappeared a minute later dragging Mama Harding behind him. In her hands was a bowl with a dish towel draped over it.

"I made you something!" Levi said as he pulled the dish towel like he was a magician revealing a trick.

"Soup?" she asked.

"Mama Harding helped me make cullen skink. I still think it's nasty, but you said you like it."

Jade's hand covered her mouth. "You made that? For me?" She was hitting gift overload today. First, Aaron had proposed, and now Levi had worked hard to make something that she loved.

She leaned down and inhaled slowly. "It smells amazing."

"Eat it! Eat it!" Levi jumped in his excitement. Thankfully, he wasn't the one carrying the soup.

Aaron laid a hand on Levi's shoulder. "Don't you have another surprise for her?"

Levi's eyes widened. "Oh! Yes!" He moved to stand side-by-side with his dad. When Levi nodded, they both knelt. Levi's shoulder was flush against Aaron's thick arm.

Jade smiled widely. This was the best day of her life, hands down. Seeing Levi act like a little man proposing to her beside his daddy melted her heart.

"Jade," Aaron began. "We love you, and we want you to become a part of our family."

Levi yelled, "Will you marry my daddy?"

Aaron turned to Levi. "I thought we decided I would do the asking and you would give her the ring."

Levi shrugged. "But I wanted to do it." He held out a ring, but she couldn't see it through her blurry tear-filled eyes.

"Yes!" Jade shouted, throwing her hands in the air.

The whole room erupted into celebratory hoots and whistles.

"Wait!" Levi shouted. "I have Skittles for you too."

Jade laughed and crouched to hug Levi. "You don't need to sweeten the pot. I already said yes."

Aaron plucked the diamond ring from Levi's fingers and took Jade's hand in his. She watched as the circle slipped onto her finger perfectly.

The second proposal may have topped the first. She was only now realizing she was going to be Mrs. Aaron Harding. She stood and looked at the crowd of Hardings waiting to congratulate her. She was going to be part of this family, and that may have been the greatest gift she'd received all day.

***

The evening was full of congratulations and hugs, and Jade hadn't even called her family yet. While she was thankful for the opportunity to help the students for a few weeks, she felt assured that her home and future was here at Blackwater.

When Aaron parked between their cabins and turned off the engine, Jade remembered the gift she'd brought back.

"Hey, I forgot that I brought a surprise for you too," she said to Levi.

"You did?" Levi sleepily asked.

"It's in my luggage. Give me a few minutes to find it, and I'll meet you at your place."

Levi could barely keep his eyes open as he and Aaron made their way inside. Jade ran to her cabin and dug through her carry-on until she felt the small plastic bag. She left the mess she'd just strewn from her luggage and sprinted to Aaron's cabin.

She stomped her feet on the porch mat before darting inside and closing the door quickly behind her to keep the cold out. A shiver ran down her spine as she removed her coat and hung it on the rack by the door.

Levi jumped from the couch where he'd been sitting. "What did you bring me?"

She opened the bag in her hand and pulled out a bracelet. Kneeling before Levi, she rubbed her fingertips over the smooth metal and twine.

"I thought about you a lot while I was away. I kept this rock with me, and I started toying around with it at my grandparents' restaurant one day." She held her fingers on both sides of the rock that rested at the center of the bracelet. "I wrapped this copper wire around the rock and shaped the rest into a bracelet. Then I added the twine that wraps along the copper and ties on the underside." She flipped the bracelet to show the two loose ends of the twine.

"I thought you might like to wear it sometimes. It's like the three of us wound up together. You're the rock at the center. I'm smooth and cool like the copper." She gave her short blonde hair a little flip that drew a small chuckle from Levi. "And your daddy is rough like the twine, but he keeps us all tied together."

Levi stared at the bracelet, and she couldn't read his expression. She should have brought something better. He'd probably been expecting a real gift. Her heart sank in his disappointment. Maybe he thought a bracelet wasn't manly or something.

Suddenly, his face scrunched up, and he threw his arms around her neck. His back rose and fell in sobs as he cried onto her shoulder.

She looked up at Aaron and silently pleaded for help. Was he just tired? Had the day been too stressful for him?

"Thank you," Levi said through his sobs.

"I'm here," Jade said as she rubbed comforting circles on his back. "I'm not going anywhere without you."

Levi leaned back and rubbed the tears from his face. "Will you put it on me?"

She tied the string around his small wrist and turned his hand over to show him the rock wound in copper and twine.

"Thanks. I love it." Levi looked up at Aaron. "Can I wear it to bed?"

"I don't see why not," Aaron said with a pat on Levi's back. "Why don't you get ready for bed?"

Levi hugged Jade again and asked, "Will you tuck me in?"

"I'd love to. You get ready, and I'll be there in a minute."

Levi ran off, and she turned to Aaron. "I thought I'd messed up."

He wrapped his strong arms around her. "I don't think you could mess up if you tried."

"You're only saying that because you love me."

Aaron leaned his mouth close to her ear to whisper, "It's all your fault. You're irresistible."

A jolt of electricity ran from the base of her neck down her spine. "You're such a romantic. You're like a teddy bear." She thought back to the first time she'd compared him to a bear. It had been a grizzly, but now she knew his sweet, comforting nature. She'd been so wrong.

"Please don't call me that in front of my brothers," Aaron asked.

Jade chuckled. "What about when we're alone?"

A low rumble emanated from Aaron's chest. "When I'm alone with you, I don't care what you call me."

The full future that lay ahead for her was still being pieced together in her mind. She would have years to spend with him, filled with moments spent alone with him as her husband, as well as joyful days spent with the family she would soon call her own.

"I want it all," she whispered, unaware that she'd spoken the words aloud until Aaron brushed his cheek against hers. The stubble was rough, but that was what she'd expected. He'd probably skipped shaving today in his rush to pick her up at the airport.

"Whatever it is you want, I'll get it for you," he said.

"No. I want to be your wife. I want to be Levi's mom. I want new sisters and brothers. I want to manage the children's programs here. I want to join the children's ministry at church. I want to teach Levi and watch him grow into a kind man like his dad." She shook her head. "I want all of these things that I can have now because of you."

She'd visited dozens of places and met hundreds of people in her life, but none of them had taken root in her life the way Aaron and his family had here at Blackwater. This place and the people she met here changed her path in life.

She hadn't known then, but God always had a plan for her to end up at home in Blackwater.

Epilogue
HUNTER

Hunter left the main house before anyone else had finished eating. There wasn't any point in sticking around. He'd get his orders from Micah later.

Hunter didn't understand group celebrations or why he needed to get excited about someone else's life events. Good for them, but he'd be just fine staying out of it.

It wasn't like Aaron and Jade's engagement was a surprise. Hunter's cousin had been talking for days about the ring he bought her.

Hunter's work was done. He'd fulfilled his obligation. He was here to work, not compliment his cousin on his taste in jewelry.

Now every woman on the ranch had a ring on their finger. Just as it should be. Dating made a man lose his mind. It was like their brains turned to mush, and all they could think about was courting and wooing women.

He parked the truck outside his cabin, the one farthest from the others, and almost made it inside before his phone rang. The calls didn't come as a surprise. When everyone else was busy, Hunter wasn't.

"Hello."

"You busy?" Jameson asked.

Hunter looked at his front door, resigned to whatever task Jameson needed taken care of while everyone else schmoozed at the main house. "No. What do you need?"

"My sister is on her way. She'll be there before me. Can you show her to Laney's old place?"

Hunter turned on the porch and looked back up the path he came. "Yeah."

"Thanks. And maybe don't scare her off. She's going through a lot right now."

Hunter remembered Jameson's sister. When was she not going through a hard time? Jameson and Felicity had escaped their parents' abuse, but only by the skin of their teeth. While Jameson had thrown himself into work when Blackwater Ranch needed an extra set of hands, his sister had disappeared without a trace. Jameson hadn't mentioned her in years. She didn't even show up to her mama's funeral.

That suited Hunter just fine. Jameson and Felicity's mother had been a walking sledgehammer, beating and destroying everything in her path. Hunter knew those people and steered clear. Luckily enough, his own destructive father had left him before either one of them got hurt. Well, physically, at least.

Felicity hadn't gotten out, and that meant she was probably just as messed up as he was. She'd been well on her way to crazy like a cornered animal the last time he'd seen her, and he doubted her life had turned into a bed of roses since then.

Hunter's hands flexed and fisted at his sides. Funny how a memory brought back the urge to break bones. That night, he hadn't cared if they were his or the other guy's. It was a good thing because there'd been enough fractures to go around.

An unfamiliar car barreled down the path toward the cabins, kicking up dust along the way.

That's what women did; they stirred up dust everywhere they went. And he needed one like he needed a hole in the head.

His cousins were fine pairing up, but Hunter was a lone wolf in more ways than one. He'd bite at anyone who got too close.

The gray sedan coming toward him might have once been silver, but years and miles had worn off the brightness.

Hunter stepped off the porch and made his way toward the car. Felicity was already out and standing at the open trunk. Her dark hair hadn't changed much, and she wore it pulled back in the same ponytail she always had when she'd been younger.

She hefted a faded blue suitcase from the back of the car. Hunter reached to help, but she was quick to jerk the luggage away from him.

"Which one?" she said. Her words were melodic and beautiful, but she said them with purpose and not a hint of pleasantry.

In most cases, he could justify someone else's foul mood by their discomfort that came with the nasty scar on his face. But Felicity's scowl had been set in place before she'd seen him, and for once, he couldn't take credit for the storm in her eyes.

Hunter pointed to the cabin beside his.

Felicity's attention followed the direction of his finger, and she closed the trunk with more force than necessary. Jerking the large bag from a rut in the dirt, she marched past him toward the cabin without a backward glance.

Hunter watched her wrestle the luggage up the trio of stairs leading to the worn porch of the cabin where she would be staying before the door slammed shut behind her with a thunk.

At least he wouldn't have to worry about a nosy neighbor. If Felicity kept her distance, they would get along just fine.

Hunter pulled his phone from his pocket and typed a text to Jameson.

She's here.

THE END

ABOUT THE AUTHOR

Mandi Blake was born and raised in Alabama where she lives with her husband and daughter, but her southern heart loves to travel. Reading has been her favorite hobby for as long as she can remember, but writing is her passion. She loves a good happily ever after in her sweet Christian romance books and loves to see her characters' relationships grow closer to God and each other.

Made in the USA
Coppell, TX
23 November 2022